CROWDED LIVES
and Other Stories
of Desperation and
Danger

CROWDED LIVES
and Other Stories of Desperation and Danger

Clark Howard

Five Star
Unity, Maine

Copyright © 2000 by Clark Howard

All rights reserved.

This collection is a work of fiction. Names, characters, places, and incidents are either the product of the author's imagination, or, if real, used fictitiously.

Five Star Mystery Series.

Published in conjunction with Tekno Books and Ed Gorman.

Cover photograph © Alan J. La Vallee

March 2000

First Edition

The text of this edition is unabridged.

Set in 11 pt. Plantin by Al Chase.

Printed in the United States on permanent paper.

Library of Congress Cataloging-in-Publication Data
Howard, Clark.
   Crowded lives and other stories of desperation and danger / by Howard Clark. — 1st ed.
     p.   cm. — (Five Star standard print mystery series)
   Contents: Introduction — Old soldiers — Hit and run — Wild things — McCulla's kid — Hanging it on a limb — New Orleans getaway — The Marksman — The color of death — Crowded lives.
   ISBN 0-7862-2366-9 (hc : alk. paper)
   1. United States — Social life and customs — 20th century — Fiction. 2. Detective and mystery stories, American. 3. Psychological fiction, American. I. Title. II. Series.
PS3558.O877 C76 2000
  813'.54—dc21   99-054226

Dedicated
with love
to my granddaughter
AMANDA LAUREN HOWARD

Contents

Introduction	7
Old Soldiers	9
Hit and Run	32
Wild Things	68
McCulla's Kid	92
Hanging It on a Limb	115
New Orleans Getaway	135
The Marksman	163
The Color of Death	178
Crowded Lives	202

Introduction

Think of a crowd and you probably think of a large group of people. An assembly of some kind. A congregation. A gathering.

And "crowded" is usually thought of as somewhere that is congested, a place of insufficient room, limited space. The term commonly means too many *people*.

But just as people can be crowded, their individual *lives* can be crowded also.

Crowded with memories of the past, problems of the present, imagined obstacles of the future. Crowded with responses, held in reserve, that can be called upon to face possible trials, answer potential questions, meet unpredictable confrontations.

Even the simplest daily life can experience such a glut of difficulties and dilemmas, plights and predicaments, and plain old low-down troubles, as to make a person wonder whether life is even worthwhile.

But most of us think it is, and we muddle through the worried hours and bad days thinking that tomorrow will be better—simply because it couldn't possibly be any worse.

The people—men, women, and children—in the following stories all have lives that are crowded with miseries and misfortune, and like the rest of us they try to get through them as best they can.

Some make it, some don't.

That's life.

Crowded life.

While serving in the Marine Corps during the Korean War, I had occasion to spend several weeks in a U.S. Naval hospital. After the war, I also had occasion to make visits to a large Veterans hospital in California. I was touched by the camaraderie among the patients in each place.

The following story is set in 1968, a time when American casualties were piling up in the Vietnam War. Every day, men with broken bodies and minds were being sent back to fill our military and naval hospitals. Some of them, unable to be mended, were discharged and transferred to veterans hospitals, where they joined other broken men from other wars: World War One, World War Two, Korea. There, men from different generations learned all over again to live together, and die together.

As soldiers always have.

Old Soldiers

It was early morning, not yet six. A surgical nurse and an orderly, both in green, walked briskly but quietly down one of the patient wings at Harry Truman Veterans Hospital. The orderly pushed a rubber-wheeled gurney that moved almost as silently as he did. At the door to Room 131, the nurse entered and turned on the light. It was a four-bed room. Sitting up on the bed to the left of the door was Ed Latham, a thin, nervous man. He had been sitting in the dark, smoking.

"Time to go, Mr. Latham," the nurse said, taking the cigarette away from him with a scolding look. The orderly pushed the gurney next to the bed and began to help Latham onto it.

Now the other three men in the room came awake and began to sit up in their respective beds. In the rear bed to the right of the room's solitary window was George Smiddy, a World War One veteran, who had recently celebrated his seventieth birthday. A tough, grizzled old man whose face looked like the Nevada desert, he had suffered most of his adult life from mustard gas poisoning contracted in the Argonne Forest campaign.

On the other side of the window from Smiddy was Frank Connor, a man in his early fifties. Wounded by a sniper on Guadalcanal, Connor was paralyzed from the waist down. A wheelchair was parked beside his bed.

Facing Latham's bed was Eugene Aidman's. Eugene was in his late thirties and the youngest man in the room. A Korean War vet, he was completely bald and had a visible metal plate in his head. On his bed table was a portable tape player that he carried wherever he went. Most of the other patients in the hospital thought he was crazy because he never listened to anything but military band music.

As their friend Latham was about to be wheeled out to surgery he was wished good luck by the other three men, each in his own way.

"Hang in there, Latham," said Aidman, rubbing his bald head.

"Try to make it back for supper," said Connor. "It's Tuesday—you wouldn't want to miss the meatloaf."

"Don't be grabbing any feels from the nurses in the operating room," old Smiddy advised. "Could make 'em drop a sponge in you."

Latham waved as he was wheeled out. "So long, fellows."

An aura of gloom settled over the room after Latham had gone. Gloom with a little anger.

"Why the hell can't they just leave him alone?" Connor

asked tensely. "He doesn't want all those damned operations. Why don't they just admit he can't be helped? Just like we can't be helped."

"I can be helped," said Aidman with a fixed stare. "I'm confident the doctors will make me see again."

"Shut up," said Connor. "You're not even blind."

"V. A. doctors are like Army doctors," Smiddy said knowingly. "They'll find a cure even if it kills you."

"This is the fifth time they've cut him open," Connor continued. "If they keep taking pieces out, he's going to be empty."

Smiddy sat up on the side of his bed. "Who's got the latrine first this morning?" he asked.

"I have," said Connor.

"Well, hop in your kiddie car and get in there. My bladder's as old as I am, you know."

"Nothing's as old as you are," Connor said.

"The pyramids are," said Aidman.

"Oh, yeah—I forgot about them."

"I'll use the bedpan," Smiddy threatened.

Connor scrambled into his chair and tooled into the bathroom.

Two hours later the three men were straggling back down the corridor from breakfast, all wearing identical blue pinstriped bathrobes over plain white cotton pajamas. Connor puffed on a foul cigar as he wheeled along. Aidman munched an apple. The two men moved at reduced speed so old Smiddy could keep up with them. But they harassed him for it.

"Jeez, Smiddy, can't you move any faster?" Aidman complained. "We're always the last ones to the rec room."

"Go ahead," Smiddy growled, "I didn't ask you to wait for me."

"The floor nurse told us to stay with you," Connor said around his cigar. "She's afraid you'll wander off and get lost."

"That's a damn lie!" Smiddy snapped. "I'd knock you down if you could stand up!"

"Hey look—" said Aidman, stopping and pointing down the corridor toward their room.

A short man in white was coming out of 131 with a cardboard box in his hands. He was a wing orderly the patients called "Undertaker" because he was responsible for cleaning out a patient's personal effects when the patients died. Looking up, he saw the three occupants of 131 stop and stare at him. He walked slowly over to them.

"Latham died on the table," he said quietly.

Old Smiddy sighed heavily and leaned a frail shoulder against the wall. Aidman, next to him, stared straight ahead and blinked back tears. Connor smacked a fist into his palm and glared up at Undertaker.

"Don't assign nobody else to his bed, you hear me? We don't want nobody else in the room with us!"

Undertaker shrugged. "I'm not sure I can do that, Connor," he said quietly. "Beds are scarce."

"I don't care!" Connor stormed. "We don't want nobody else in with us!" He took the cigar out of his mouth and his voice softened. "Look, it just ain't worth it. You get a new guy in your room, live with him for a year or two while those meatballs over in surgery take him apart piece by piece, you get to liking him, he gets to be your friend, then *bang*—" he put the cigar back in his mouth and slammed his fist into his palm again, "—the guy's dead and you've lost a friend." A pitiful expression settled on his face. Like Aidman, his eyes moistened. "I've lost enough friends," he said quietly. "I don't want to lose any more."

Aidman patted Connor on the shoulder and pushed him

toward their room. Smiddy shuffled along behind them. Undertaker, left alone in the hall, stared sadly after them.

Two days later the men were out on the field of a vast cemetery of symmetrically placed crosses. They stood beside a freshly covered grave with a single wreath on it.

"Another casualty," Smiddy said quietly. He looked around, his eyes sweeping the rows of crosses. "When I first came to this hospital back in '21, there were only sixteen graves here. Now it's like the remains of a battlefield."

"It *is* the remains of a battlefield," Aidman said.

Connor looked up from his chair. "The chaplain's already prayed over Latham, but don't you think we should say something too? Being as how we were his only friends?"

"Good idea," said Aidman. "You do it, Smiddy."

Smiddy scowled. For a long moment he looked at the grave in contemplation. Then he cleared his throat and spoke.

"Old soldiers never die. They just fade away."

After Smiddy said it, Aidman slipped a cassette into his tape player and turned it on. The military band strains of "The Stars and Stripes Forever" began to play. The three of them came to attention as the music wafted over the rows of graves.

Life—and death—went on at Harry Truman Veterans Hospital. A month passed. Room 131 now had a hand-lettered sign on the outside of its door: NEW MAGAZINES FOR SALE—HALF PRICE. Undertaker looked at the sign in disgust as he parked his mail cart and carried two large bundles, one of magazines, the other of bills for the magazines.

"Good day, orderly," Connor greeted him. "Put the magazines right over there—" he pointed to Latham's old bed, now stripped of linen, its bare mattress covered by the display of a wide variety of magazines "—and toss that bundle of bills in the incinerator."

"How long do you think you can get away with this?" Undertaker asked. "You must owe a thousand dollars to these publishers."

Connor drew up in his chair indignantly. "Me? Owe money? I don't owe nothing to nobody. If you'll look at the address labels, you'll see that all the magazines *and* the bills are made out to O.C. Cupant in Room 131 of the Harry Truman Veterans Hospital. O.C. Cupant spells 'Occupant' and federal law states that people don't have to pay for anything sent to 'Occupant.' It's not my fault if the magazines are too dumb to catch on."

"I still think you're gonna get caught," said Undertaker. "You're using the mails to defraud."

"Big deal," said Aidman. "So what if he gets caught? What are they gonna do, send him to prison? In order to do that, they first gotta build a new prison—one with wheelchair ramps and wider cells."

Undertaker dumped the bundle of new magazines on the bed. "Well, anyway, you're gonna have to find someplace else to display your wares. This bed's gonna be occupied starting tomorrow."

"You little rat," Smiddy growled from his bed. "We said we didn't want nobody else in here."

"It's not my fault. There's a shortage of beds. Anyway, it won't be for long. This guy's a transfer from Tokyo General. His lungs were damaged by napalm fumes in 'Nam. They're not purifying his blood like they should. The army docs have only given him a couple of months. He's coming here to die 'cause he's got no family."

The three patients raised collective hell. "Why put him in here with us? Find someplace else for him! Pitch a tent out on the cemetery and put him in there—that's where he's headed anyway! Give us a break!"

The new patient's name was Steve Crane. He was in his mid-twenties, still in uniform, wearing sergeant's stripes. Undertaker brought him in one afternoon when the men were out. "Have a seat on the chair there while I make up your bed," he said.

The young soldier leaned his duffel bag against the wall and sat down. He was tired from the long flight from Tokyo. Turning in the chair, he looked out the window at the vast cemetery. His expression was one of resignation: he knew he was dying and apparently had accepted it.

While Undertaker was making the bed, the room's other three occupants straggled in. Each one stopped and stared at Crane. He stared back at them, curious about these men with whom he would spend the final days of his life. Finally Connor wheeled forward, all business—he didn't even offer to shake hands.

"I'm Connor, World War Two. That's Aidman, Korea. The old guy is Smiddy, from the Great War. We take turns having first call on the latrine. The TV is rented. If you want a share of that, it'll cost you three bucks a week and every fourth day will be yours— otherwise you have to watch what we watch. Aside from that, there ain't no other rules: it's live and let live, so to speak. But you ought to know from the start that we ain't very sociable. Get my meaning?"

Crane's eyes narrowed slightly. "I get the picture. Don't worry. I'm not looking to make any lifelong friends—so to speak."

Aidman and Smiddy went to their beds without saying anything.

Connor turned his wheelchair toward his own bed. Crane

resumed staring out the window. Undertaker, finishing up with the bed, looked from Connor to Aidman to Smiddy. "Nice guys," he muttered.

"Mind your own business, orderly," Connor snapped.

"Yeah, this is between soldiers," said Smiddy.

"I don't need nobody to fight my battles," Crane told Undertaker.

The beleaguered orderly threw up his hands in surrender and left.

After a moment, Crane opened his duffel bag and removed a small-framed photo of a dark-haired pretty young woman. He wiped it off on his sleeve and set it on his bed table. Then he loosened his tie and stretched out on the bed, staring at the ceiling.

Connor, Smiddy, and Aidman all looked at the photo, exchanged glances and shrugged.

"I thought you said the guy had no family," Aidman accused Undertaker in the corridor after supper that night. "Who the hell's the girl in the picture—his doctor?"

"Man, I don't know who she is," Undertaker demurred. "All I know is what's on the guy's card. If you want to know who she is, why don't you ask him?"

"That's personal," Connor said. "We ain't getting personal with this guy."

"You find out for us," Smiddy said to Undertaker.

"Me? How can *I* find out?"

"The way you find out everything else, snooping in the files. Find out which outfit he was in, then cross-check the records and find somebody else who was in the same outfit. It's a big hospital—somebody must know him."

"What does it matter who she is anyway?"

"It matters," said Aidman. "If he's got family or a girlfriend, he's got no business dying with us. He should be made

Old Soldiers

to die with somebody he knows."

The trio went on into 131 and Connor turned on the TV set. It was his night to have possession of the remote-control unit, and therefore the programming. But it was their custom to watch *The Six O'Clock News* no matter whose turn it was. This was 1968, during the heat of the Vietnam War, and night after night, for some perverse reason not even they understood, they were drawn to watch the carnage reported in the news.

"Time for 'This is Your War,' " Connor said. "The continuing story of men in battle, yesterday's heroes, today's cripples."

As the commentator began talking about the bombing of Hanoi, Crane got off his bed, put on his robe and slippers, and left the room. The others didn't pay much attention. The next evening when Aidman turned on the same news program, Crane left again. This time the men noticed. On the third night, when he left still again, they knew. "It's the war news," said Smiddy. "It gets to him."

"Tough," said Connor. "Turn it up, will you?"

"Probably reminds him he's dying," offered Aidman.

"We're all dying," Connor told him. "Some of us are just doing it faster than others."

Aidman went to the door and looked down the hall. He saw Steve Crane sitting alone on the stairs. Aidman felt the metal plate in his head. He couldn't help feeling a little disturbed.

The next day the three men were playing cards in the rec room when Undertaker came in.

"I found out who the girl in the picture is. She's a French nurse he fell for in the hospital in Saigon. A guy being trained on a new leg over in Prosthetics was in the hospital there with him. He said Crane and this nurse fell for each other real heavy—a kind of love-at-first-sight thing. Her name is Ceil Chatalier. Everybody in the hospital knew about it. They spent all their free time together. When Crane was transferred to Tokyo General, the girl hitched rides on supply planes to go see him on weekends. They were putting through the paper work to get permission to be married. Then Crane learned he was dying, the Tet offensive began, and the nurse was evacuated, probably back to France. Crane's been trying for months to find her—writing letters to the French government, the French medical associations, hospitals in Paris—but so far no trace of her."

"He doesn't still want to marry her, does he?" asked Aidman.

Undertaker shook his head. "Not according to this guy in Prosthetics. He just wants to write her a letter before he dies. Or maybe talk to her on an overseas call."

"Don't seem like much to ask," Aidman reflected.

Smiddy shook his head. "A damn shame he can't find her."

"Yeah, war is hell," Connor commented. "It's your deal, Aidman."

A few mornings later Undertaker came hurrying into the solarium where all four of the men were sunning. He had an official-looking envelope for Crane, who was a little off to himself from the others. "You're not supposed to get this until the regular mail run," he said, "but it's all the way from France and it looks important."

Crane tore open the letter. But his expression of anticipation dissolved to disappointment as he read it. Finally he sighed quietly but very deeply, crumpled the letter into a ball and dropped it into the wastebasket, and left the solarium.

Undertaker retrieved the letter and read it.

"It's from the French Medical Corps," he said. "Ceil Chatalier was discharged from the service in Paris six months ago. There's no record of her present whereabouts."

The men all looked a little downcast, and this time there was no gruff remark from Connor.

That evening, when it was time for the news, Smiddy picked up the remote-control unit and switched on the set. Crane as usual got up and started for the door.

"Hey, kid, you don't have to leave," said Smiddy. "I've decided to watch *The Hollywood Squares* tonight."

Connor stared at him incredulously. "Are you crazy? *The Hollywood Squares?*"

"You don't have to do me any favors, pop," said Crane.

"To answer *your* question," Smiddy said archly to Connor, "no, I'm not crazy. And for *your* information," he said to Crane, "I'm not doing you any favors, *sonny*. It's my night to use the television and I've decided to watch something besides the damned bloody war news. To hell with both of you if you don't like it." And he turned on *The Hollywood Squares*.

Connor and Crane looked at each other.

"All right!" Connor said indignantly. "If that's the way you feel about it!" He flipped off the bed into his chair and wheeled out of the room.

"I'm not staying either," Crane said. "I don't need no buddy-buddy charity from anybody." He stalked off in a different direction down the hall from Connor—but presently Connor stopped and spun his chair around. "Hey, kid!" he hollered at Crane.

Crane paused and looked back. "Yeah?"

"To hell with that old fool. Come over to the canteen and I'll buy you a beer."

Crane thought about it for a moment. Then he nodded curtly. "Why not?"

As Crane and Connor went off down the hall together, Aidman, watching from the door of 131, turned to Smiddy and winked. "It worked."

Smiddy merely grunted. He was staring at the television, engrossed in the game show he had turned on.

A couple of days later, the four men were wandering around the grounds together. Aidman had his tape player, with a cassette of "Colonel Bogey's March" playing on low volume.

"You know," Smiddy told Crane, "we might be able to help you find that girl of yours. I've got a friend who owns a bistro in Lyons. He went back over there after the war and married a French woman. He's probably got a lot of contacts that he could ask for help. Be a lot easier than writing all those letters and waiting for answers."

"Sure," said Connor, "and I've got a buddy who's a TWA pilot and flies to Paris all the time. Maybe he could check some of those hospitals that never replied."

"You guys are really desperate to get rid of me, aren't you?" Crane chided, only half in jest. "You think if I locate Ceil I'll find some way to go to France and then you can have the room to yourselves again."

"Well, it would be nice to watch *The Six O'Clock News* again," Connor admitted. "*Hollywood Squares* depresses me. All those happy people winning all that money.'

"You're just sore because you're broke and crippled," said Aidman.

"Not at all," Connor retorted. "I take pride in being broke and crippled. It's very gratifying to know I'm a permanent burden to the taxpayers."

Smiddy got serious again. "What do you say, kid? Do you want us to try and help you find your girl?"

Crane nodded, embarrassed. "Thanks," he said quietly.

"Don't mention it," Smiddy said, slapping him on the back. "Us old soldiers got to stick together."

That evening, when Crane had gone to the movie in the rec room, Aidman said, "You know, what he said earlier, about finding some way to go to France, got me to thinking. Suppose he *could* go over there, either to see her or to look for her if we don't find her first?"

"Where would he get the money to do that?" Smiddy asked. "Hell, the kid's practically broke, just like us. All he's got is his lousy disability pension."

"Yeah," said Connor, "and traveling to Europe ain't exactly cheap—you're talking about a lot of bucks."

"What if we all chipped in?"

"Still wouldn't have enough," Smiddy said. "Even with Connor's magazine money, we wouldn't have enough."

"Well, maybe there's another way," Aidman said. "With this plate in my head, I could go at any time. And I've still got my G. I. life insurance. Ten thousand bucks."

Smiddy and Connor exchanged looks.

"What the hell are you getting at?" Connor asked suspiciously.

"If you're talking suicide, forget it," Smiddy growled. "Soldiers don't do that."

"I'm not talking about suicide," said Aidman. "I'm not even talking about really dying. But if we could get the right paperwork going to make the government *think* I died—I mean, it's a big hospital, guys must cash in every day. Who'd notice an extra set of papers?"

Now Smiddy and Connor exchanged interested looks.

★ ★ ★ ★ ★

The next day, when Undertaker was making his mail run, Smiddy fell in beside him in the corridor. "Mind if I walk along with you for a while?" he asked with a smile.

Undertaker looked at the old man suspiciously. "I thought you didn't like me."

Smiddy feigned surprise. "What in the world made you think that?"

Undertaker shrugged. "You're always calling me names."

"Well, maybe I just never really appreciated you before. I didn't realize you had so much responsibility around here."

"My job's not easy," Undertaker admitted. "I work a lot harder than the doctors do."

"I'm beginning to realize that. I just found out you're the one who does most of the work when a patient dies."

"We call it 'expires,' " Undertaker corrected. "When a patient expires."

"Yes, of course, expires. How nice. You have to take care of all that paperwork, don't you?"

"Well, *I* don't exactly take care of it. What I do is collect all the information so the records section can take care of it."

"What do you mean? What information?"

"I pick up the death certificate from the doctor on duty. I take the patient's medical file from the ward. I get a claim certificate from the insurance office, and I take it all to the records section for processing."

Smiddy played dumb. "Processing?"

"That's when the records section notarizes the death certificate, closes out the medical file, and sends in the claim form for the expired patient's government insurance."

"I see. Then whoever his beneficiary is gets an insurance check?"

"Right."

"A very efficient system," Smiddy said, nodding. "Nice and simple."

Undertaker smiled, pleased. "You want me to tell you about all I have to do when a patient is transferred?"

"No, I don't," Smiddy growled. He had learned all he needed to know. "I don't have time to stand around and listen to you brag about how important you are. Expires! Sounds like you're talking about some damned license plate. Get away from me, you little rat!"

Now that they knew the procedure, the men put their plan to work.

Connor wheeled up to a desk in the hospital bank and smiled at the girl on duty. "I'm a new patient just transferred in from Walter Reed Medical Center. I'd like to open a checking account, please."

"All right, sir. What is your name, please?"

"Cupant," Connor said. "O.C. Cupant."

While Connor was doing that, Smiddy shuffled into the insurance office. "I need a change of beneficiary form," he told the clerk. "I'm outliving all my relatives."

And in another corridor well away from Room 131, Aidman slipped into an orderly supply closet and used the badge-making machine to punch out a hospital nameplate: O.C. Cupant. On his way out, he stole a white orderly's uniform.

Later in the day, Connor wheeled past the nurses' station on their own wing and stopped at the drinking fountain. At the opposite end of the corridor Smiddy slipped over to the fire alarm and pulled it. A loud bell began ringing. All the nurses at the station immediately rushed out to search for the fire. During the confusion, Connor wheeled behind the counter, opened a desk drawer, and tore off several sheets from a pad of blank death certificates. Spinning his chair around, he then pulled open a file drawer and quickly snatched out Aidman's medical record. He was back out in the corridor, the stolen articles under his bathrobe, when the nurses determined that it had been a false alarm and returned to their stations.

On his way back to 131, Connor stuck his head in the door of another patient's room. "Hey, Lenny, let me borrow your portable typewriter for an hour, will you?" Lenny acquiesced and, with the typewriter on his lap, Connor was wheeling home when Aidman came hurrying up to him.

"It's the kid," he said urgently. "Undertaker found him unconscious on the floor of the room. They've got him in the trauma section trying to bring him back."

The men waited tensely in the corridor outside the trauma unit.

"He was white as a ghost when I found him," Undertaker said. "I thought for sure he'd bought it."

"You mean you thought he'd expired," Smiddy said sarcastically.

Presently a doctor emerged. "He's coming out of it," he told them, "but it was close. His lungs are deteriorating badly. I don't think he has more than a few weeks left."

The men started back to their room. "We're going to have to hustle if we expect to pull this off in time," Connor said.

"We can make it," Smiddy told him confidently. "We're almost ready. You sent in the form naming O.C. Cupant your beneficiary, right?" he said to Aidman. Aidman nodded. "And you," Smiddy turned to Connor, "got the blank death certificate and the medical file. The bank account is open. All we need now is that claim certificate from the insurance office."

Connor looked at Aidman. "That's your job."

"I know. I'll do it tomorrow morning. I just hope it works."

"It will."

They heard running footsteps and turned to see Undertaker hurrying toward them. "In the excitement I forgot why I went into your room in the first place," he said when he caught up. "I was bringing this telegram that came for Connor."

Frowning, Connor opened the envelope. He read the message, then looked up smiling. "It's from my buddy, Al, the TWA pilot. He's located the girl. She's working at Notre Dame Hospital in Vitry, just outside Paris."

The next morning the three men moved casually along the corridor near the insurance office. As usual, they were dressed in bathrobes, but now Aidman had a towel around his neck under the robe collar. When they were just past the insurance office door, they paused as if having a conversation, looking around to make sure no one was paying any attention to them. Then Aidman whipped off the robe and towel, revealing underneath an orderly uniform complete with name badge. Connor reached under his own robe and passed him a curly black wig which he flopped onto his metal-plated skull. "How do I look?" he asked nervously.

"Like Burt Reynolds."

"Really?" Aidman said, preening.

"Get in there," Smiddy growled, pushing him.

Aidman straightened his shoulders and sauntered into the office. "Morning," he said to a woman at the first desk. He took a slip of paper from his pocket. "I need a claim certificate for a guy named Aidman, first name Eugene. Patient number 1172-307. Expired yesterday of a brain hemorrhage."

The woman took the slip and checked her files. "Are you new?" she asked.

"No, I've been here for a while. I usually work nights. I'm filling in for a guy."

"Here it is," she said, pulling out a card. "Ten thousand dollars. Just let me put a date on it and stamp it. Expired yesterday? You have the death certificate?"

"Yeah." Aidman handed her the fake certificate Connor had typed up. It felt a little odd processing the paperwork on his own death.

When the woman finally handed him the validated certificate, she glanced at his name badge. "Cupant. I knew a fellow named Cupant once. In college."

"No kidding?" Aidman said, immediately intrigued. "Did he get a lot of mail?"

"I don't know. Why do you ask?"

"Oh, no reason." Aidman shrugged. Going back down the hall, he was joined by Connor and Smiddy, who gave him his robe to put back on.

Snatching off the wig, he raised his eyebrows maniacally and said gleefully, "O.C. Cupant strikes again!"

A few days later, Steve Crane returned to Room 131 from his stay in the recuperation ward. The men welcomed him with a hand-lettered sign that read BACK FROM THE DEAD, a bottle of champagne, and Aidman's cassette player turned on to a tape of "It's A Grand Old Flag." Crane was pleased. It was genuine evidence of his acceptance by the men: he was one of them now.

But all was not going well with their plan. During the celebration, Undertaker came to the door and motioned Connor into the hall.

"I don't know what you guys are up to," he said, "but I

think you ought to know that the FBI was here a little while ago. They were looking into an account in the name of O.C. Cupant that was opened at the hospital bank. They also talked to administration about a government insurance check that's been sent here: somebody's trying to beat the government out of ten grand. They didn't catch on until after the check was mailed, so they couldn't stop it earlier. Anyway, when it comes in I'm not supposed to deliver it to Room 131. I'm supposed to turn it over to administration and then the FBI guys are gonna come back out."

Connor nodded solemnly. "I appreciate the tip," he said.

Undertaker shrugged. "Don't mention it. All's it could do is cost me my job."

Later when Crane was taking a nap, Connor met the other two men in the snack shop and told them what Undertaker had said. "It looks like they've got us," he concluded dejectedly. "They're gonna grab the check before it even gets to us."

"Even if they didn't," Aidman said, "we'd still be up the creek. With them onto the bank account, there's no way we could cash a ten-thousand-dollar check."

The men fell into a silent depression. Then they heard a voice say: "Sounds like you guys got a problem."

They looked around and saw Undertaker.

"You spying on us, you little rat?" Smiddy said threateningly.

"Not really," said Undertaker. "But I think I've figured out what you're up to. I, uh, thought maybe I could help."

"We don't need your help," Smiddy growled.

"Wait a minute," said Aidman, curious. "How do you think you can help us, Undertaker?"

"I'm the one who sorts the mail, so I'm the one who'll be getting the check," he reminded them. "Plus which I've got an established bank account outside the hospital, so I can cash it."

The three men at the table exchanged silent glances. Their expressions changed to interest.

"Sit down," said Connor, pulling up a chair.

The orderly came over and sat down. "There's one condition," he said.

"What is it?" Smiddy asked suspiciously.

"I don't want you to call me Undertaker any more. Or a little rat. My name's Melvin. I want to be called Melvin."

They all stared at him as the simplicity as well as the complexity of his request registered on them. Then Connor and Aidman looked at Smiddy, who was the one most adamantly against outsiders. Civilians, as he called them. Smiddy studied the young man for a moment longer. Finally he extended his hand.

"Welcome to the squad, Melvin," he said.

The check arrived, and Undertaker—now Melvin—took it, bearing Connor's O.C. Cupant endorsement, to his bank and cashed it. He brought the money back to Room 131. "You'll have to hurry," he told the men. "I got called into the administrator's office on the way back. The FBI can't understand why the check hasn't shown up yet. They're on their way over to question you guys—and me—right now."

Connor nodded crisply and turned to Aidman. "Reservation made?"

"Check. Non-stop to Paris. The plane leaves at two. He'll have to be at the airport by one-thirty."

"We'll need some way to get him off the hospital grounds without attracting attention."

"I can check out a hospital van," Melvin said.

"Good! Get it and meet us at the south corridor door."

Melvin hurried away. Connor wheeled across the room. "You guys pack his things," he said to Smiddy and Aidman. "I'll go to the solarium and get him."

Five minutes later, Connor returned with a puzzled Steve Crane. "What's going on? What are you guys doing with my things?"

"We found your girl, son," Smiddy told him. "And we're buying you a ticket to Paris."

Crane was dumfounded. He stared at them incredulously.

"I sent her a cable an hour ago," Aidman told him. "She's meeting your plane in the morning."

"This must be some kind of dream," Crane said.

"It's real, buddy," Connor said nervously. "But you've got to hurry. There's a van waiting outside to take you to the airport. Come on, get dressed, hurry up—"

When Crane had his uniform on they hustled him out to the van. To their surprise, old Smiddy climbed in with him. "I'm going to the airport to see him off," he announced.

"Are you crazy? In your robe and pajamas?"

Smiddy as usual was adamant. "I'm going."

"Hell, we'll *all* go then," Connor said.

They collapsed Connor's wheelchair and put it in the rear of the van. Melvin drove them off the hospital grounds. On the way out the gate, they passed a car with two men in the front seat. "Those are the FBI guys," Melvin whispered.

On the way to the airport, Aidman handed Crane an envelope. "A thousand bucks," he said. "That'll pay for your ticket. First class. And there's a little extra that we packed in your duffel bag."

"Where the hell did you guys come up with that kind of money?" Crane asked suspiciously.

"We chipped in," Connor said over his shoulder.

"That's right," said Smiddy. "Even Melvin."

Crane frowned. "Melvin?"

"That's me," said the orderly. "My name wasn't really Undertaker."

Back at the hospital the two FBI agents went looking for Melvin to question him about the check.

"He signed out a van to take somebody to the airport," another orderly told them.

The agents hurried to Room 131. They found empty drawers standing open in one of the bureaus and the rest of the occupants missing.

Quickly they got back to their car and raced to the airport.

The group hurrying to the TWA check-in gate received more than a few curious glances. Understandably. A shuffling old man, a younger bald man with a metal plate in his head, and a cripple in a wheelchair, dressed in pajamas and robes, accompanied by a hospital orderly and a young army sergeant carrying a duffel bag. But the group didn't care; their only interest was getting their friend on the plane.

Their farewell was brief, a little awkward. "This is a pretty high price to pay for a lousy hospital room," Crane said. "I—I guess I won't be seeing you guys again." His voice choked a little.

"Sure you will," Smiddy assured him. "Old soldiers all go to the same place when they fade away. We'll be along—all of us."

Crane shook hands with each of then, and with Melvin.

Outside, the FBI men cruised the airport until they spotted the hospital van in front of the TWA terminal. Quickly they parked next to it, collected two airport security men and hurried inside. Methodically they began checking departure gates.

At the departure gate for the Paris flight, Steve Crane's four friends watched from an observation window as the big

Boeing 747 taxied out to the runway and took off. They watched the plane until it was out of sight. Their faces were sad. But happy-sad.

As they turned to leave, they found the FBI agents and airport security waiting for them.

Smiddy snorted audibly, squared his frail old shoulders, and shuffled proudly past them.

Connor lighted a cigar, said, "Home, Jeeves," and sat back as Melvin pushed him along behind Smiddy.

Taking the tape player out of his robe pocket and switching it on to "When Johnny Comes Marching Home," Aidman brought up the rear.

The sport of boxing has been part of my life since I was a young boy working after school sweeping up at the Midwest Athletic Club in Chicago. Later I boxed for it in junior club fights. When I was grown and back from the Korean War, I did publicity work for the old International Boxing Club. After I moved to Las Vegas, I wrote a monthly column for The Ring magazine.

I love boxing, I follow no other sport. During my life, I have met, among others, Joe Louis, Tony Zale, Rocky Graziano, Kid Gavilan, Carl "Bobo" Olson, Muhammad Ali, Sonny Liston, Floyd Patterson, and the great Sugar Ray Robinson. But the fighters I came to know best were the ones whose names nobody today would recognize. They never won titles, were never ranked contenders, never earned the big money. They were just fighters, who did the only thing they knew how to do.

Like the one in this story.

Hit and Run

The body was found sixty feet up an alley behind the Midwest Athletic Club, on the west side of Chicago. Ironically, it was lying up against the back wall of a hospital that fronted on the next street over. Rubino, the homicide sergeant from the 12th Street station, found definite signs that the body had been dragged all the way from the mouth of the alley to where it was found.

"What killed him?" he asked Grimes, the assistant medical examiner assigned to the morgue wagon.

"He was stomped to death by a gorilla," Grimes said.

"Cute," Rubino remarked. "Does the coroner know you say funny things like that about poor unfortunate homicide victims?"

"Sure. All my witty sayings are straight from the coroner's handbook." Grimes rose from where he had been kneeling beside the corpse. "All I know so far is that the man's got contusions all over his body. I've noted them on his face, neck, upper torso, and calves. I assume when I get him downtown and strip him I'll find similar marks on the rest of his body. But as for the cause of death, I wouldn't even guess until I can cut him open and see what he looks like inside. Okay?"

"Sure, okay. But do you think a good educated guess might be that he was dragged by a car from the street down to here?"

Grimes looked down the alley, glanced at the corpse again, and shrugged. "Very possible," he allowed.

Rubino turned to another detective. "Radio the lab and have them send out a team. And tell the uniforms to rope off the alley at both ends. If this was a hit-and-run, maybe we can get some tire tracks or something." He looked back at Grimes, said, "Thanks, Doc," and started to walk away.

"Haven't you forgotten something?" Grimes said. Rubino turned back, frowning. "The Jackson-Handley fight last night," Grimes reminded him. "We had a small wager."

"Oh, yeah," Rubino said, disgruntled. He took a five-dollar bill from his pocket and handed it to Grimes. "You realize that gambling is illegal in this city, don't you?"

"So's homicide," said Grimes. "Get to work."

The Jackson-Handley heavyweight fight the previous night had been matched three weeks earlier. Dave Handley, one of the contestants, had alighted from a city bus just one block from where the homicide victim had been found, and crossed the street to enter the Midwest Athletic Club. Dave had on an old leather jacket that was worn and cracked in places, and a folded-up *Sun-Times* was sticking out of his pocket. He looked anything but prosperous as he ignored the elevator and took the stairs two at a time up to the second floor. On the way he passed a couple of palookas.

"Hey, Dave, you doing your road work?" one of them yelled. Handley waved at them without answering.

Upstairs, Dave entered a large, open gymnasium. It was crowded and noisy. Fighters were sparring in the two training rings; others were shadow boxing in front of full-length mirrors, working on speed bags, jumping rope. Lounging on a row of wooden bleachers against one wall were a dozen spectators. There was a peculiar smell in the air: sweat and cigar smoke.

Dave began threading his way down the length of the room. As he moved along, he was greeted here and there by various fighters and trainers.

"Hey, Davey-boy, howareya?"

"Dave, long time no see—"

"Big Dave, whatdayaknow, whatdayasay?"

Dave returned each greeting with a word, a wave, and a friendly punch. Gradually he made his way back to a door marked PRIVATE. He started to enter, then paused and looked over at a fighter in his early 20s, some ten years younger than his own age. The fighter was lean and muscular; he was doing strenuous sit-ups with his feet elevated. For a brief, suspended moment as he watched the younger man, Dave's expression became wistful, melancholy, as if he were remembering.

After a moment, Dave went through the door into a small, seedy reception room containing half a dozen wooden chairs, a table littered with old copies of *The Ring* magazine, and some empty pop bottles in a butt can. At a desk next to the inner office door sat a thin, harried-looking woman wearing a print dress just a touch too large for her skinny frame. She had a nervous habit of constantly checking the top button of her blouse. "Yes, may I help you?" she asked.

"Leo sent word he wanted to see me," Dave said.

"What's your name, please?"

"Joe Louis."

"Just a minute, Mr. Louis." She went into the inner office, then returned a moment later. "You may go in, Mr. Louis."

At a hopelessly cluttered desk in the office sat Leo Marvel, a partly bald, chain-smoking fight promoter who never smiled. Next to his desk was a large cardboard box containing a shaggy alley cat nursing five tiny kittens. Marvel looked up at Dave with a scowl.

"You a wise guy or something, Handley, with the Joe Louis stuff? It's hard enough to keep a secretary around this snake pit without guys like you putting her on."

Dave sat down, bobbing his chin at the kittens. "I see you're a family man now."

"That ain't funny, Dave," Leo said somberly. "I been a family man all of my life. I don't have to bring in no alley cat for a family."

"Sorry," Dave said contritely. "I didn't mean it like a crack."

"The cat didn't have no place else to go. I couldn't let it have kittens in the alley, could I?"

" 'Course not. That was nice of you, Leo. What'd you want to see me about?"

"What are you doing now? You working?" As he spoke, Leo rose and came around the desk.

"I'm unloading trucks in the warehouses over on Roosevelt Road."

Leo stood in front of him and examined a furrow of scar tissue under one eyebrow. "That's day work, ain't it?"

Dave shrugged self-consciously. "Yeah, kind of. I mean,

you got to be hired every morning just like on the docks, but if you're steady they get to know you. I get on most every day."

Leo fingered Dave's nose where it had been broken twice, and felt some thickening in the cartilage of his right ear. "Day work is still day work," he declared. "It's for winos, junkies, and hoboes."

"Sure, okay," Dave said, pushing Marvel's hand away. "Look, what do you want, Leo?"

"How long since you had a fight?" the promoter asked, returning to his chair.

"A year ago August. Why?"

"Fourteen months," Leo said reflectively, pursing his lips. "What do you weigh?"

"Two-ten, two-twelve. Why?"

"Can you get down to one-ninety-five in three weeks?"

"Sure. Why?"

"Lester Jackson, that's why. The black kid that won the gold medal in the Pan American Games last summer—and would have won the same thing in the Olympics if we'd sent a team to Moscow. He's making his pro debut on a card I'm putting together at the Stadium in three weeks. I need a good trial horse to throw in with him."

"Why me?" Dave asked.

"Two reasons. One, you're white. Two, he can take you."

"What makes you so sure?"

"That he can take you?"

"No, Leo, that I'm white," Dave said sarcastically.

"Wise guy. He can take you because you're a sucker for a scientific left. That's why you're 42 and 18. This kid's got the classiest left since Ray Robinson." Leo leaned forward and folded his hands on the cluttered desk. "The match'll be six rounds. The TV people are gonna televise the main go plus Jackson's debut. I'll give you fifteen hundred."

"If I take him, will you throw some steady work my way?"

"You won't take him, believe me. You want the slot or don't you?"

"Yeah. Sure, I want it."

"Fine. I'll have the contracts drawn up tomorrow for the state athletic commission. And I'll open up a locker for you. Start training." Leo took a roll from his pocket and peeled off some bills. "Two hundred now, the rest after."

Handley took the money and left. On his way out of the gym, he pulled the *Sun-Times* from his back pocket. It was folded to the 'Help Wanted' ads. Some of them were circled in pencil. Without looking at them, Dave threw the paper in a trashcan.

Down in the West Side tenderloin, in a large, old-fashioned pool hall, Dave found a pale, pink-eyed mulatto named, appropriately, Pink. He was lounging on a bench, watching two punks trying to out-hustle each other at nine-ball. Dave sat down beside him. "Hey, Pink, how goes it?"

"Dave, my man!" Pink said with a smile. "I ain't seen you in months."

"I been like semi-retired," Dave said. "Waiting for the right match to come along, you know?"

"Yeah," said Pink, "that's about what I been doing too: waiting for something to come along."

"Listen, I got a fight lined up. I need some stuff to work with. You still got all your training gear?"

"Yeah, sure." Pink's expression turned eager. "Who you matched with?"

"Lester Jackson."

Pink's eyebrows went up. "That kid from the Pan Am Games? He's dynamite, Dave."

Handley shrugged. "I think I can take him. What about

the gear? I'll pay you a hundred to let me use it for three weeks. And fifty a week for you to train me. Deal?"

"Deal," Pink quickly agreed.

"Meet me at the gym at nine tomorrow." Dave glanced at a clock on the wall. "Got to run, man."

He rode a bus back to the neighborhood where he lived, and went into a large supermarket on the corner. Going down one of the aisles, he took a cellophane package from a shelf, then went to a table filled with small potted plants and selected one of those. Paying for his purchases, he hurried down the street to a shabby four-story gray-stone building and ran up to the third floor rear where he lived. As soon as he got inside the door, a woman's voice said, "Dave? Did you remember to stop at the store for bread?"

Handley hit himself lightly on the forehead with the heel of his hand. He walked into the kitchen.

"Dave—?" The voice belonged to Dora, his wife. She was a year older than him, 35, but she looked 40. Her hair was long and fine, already gray-streaked. There was a worn, dissatisfied look about her, as if she constantly waged long struggles for things she never got.

As Dave came in, Dora glanced at the grocery bag in his hand and said, "You remembered the bread. Good."

"I didn't remember the bread," Dave said. "I'm sorry."

"What's that, then?" she asked.

Dave pulled out the cellophane package. "Marshmallow cookies. Your favorite kind." Then he pulled out the little plant. "And this."

Dora smiled a wide smile. "You got a job!"

"Yeah. Well, sort of."

Dora's smile contracted. "What do you mean, 'sort of'?"

"Look, I don't want you to get upset, but Leo Marvel sent word around this morning that he wanted to see me—"

"You went to the gym?" Dora said tightly. "Instead of looking for a job?"

"Just to see what he wanted, honey—"

Dora put the cookies and plant on the table and pushed them away from her as if they were contaminated. "You promised me, Dave," she said, her words an accusation. "You swore to me. You said if I came back to you that you'd give it up for good. Now just tell me one thing: did you take a fight?"

"No, I didn't take no fight," Dave lied. "I just said I'd consider one. I wanted to talk it over with you first."

"There's nothing to talk over. We're getting along fine without you fighting."

"Yeah, we sure are," Dave said, looking around the shabby little apartment.

"Things will improve once you get a steady job."

"Yeah, well what if I *can't* get a steady job?"

"Then we'll have to make it the way we're doing now. I'll be getting a raise at the laundry soon, and with what you make at the loading dock—"

"I'm sick of the loading dock, Dora," he snapped. "You know what the loading dock job is? Day work, that's what! It's for winos, and junkies and hoboes. I'm no bum, Dora."

"You're an over-the-hill fighter, Dave," she snapped back. "That's the same thing!"

For a moment they faced each other in a strange silence that saturated the room. Their eyes locked in a kind of unyielding defiance. Dora, as usual, turned out to be the stronger of the two; Dave looked away first. Then suspicion clouded Dora's face.

"You did say you just *talked* about a fight today, didn't you?"

"Yeah, that's all," Dave lied again.

As Dave spoke, almost as if in punishment for his second

lie, there was a loud knock at the door. Dora stepped into the other room and opened the door. It was Pink.

"Dora, listen," he said, "tell Dave I'll be a little late at the gym in the morning. I got to stop at a shoe shop and get a chin strap sewed on the headgear he's gonna be using—"

"Pink—" Dave said urgently, coming in quickly from the kitchen. But it was too late; Dora had turned to face him, hurt and anger in her expression. After a moment, she shook her head: a combination of helplessness, frustration, and defeat. She went over to the couch where she had earlier left her coat and purse. She put the coat on, picked up the purse.

"I'll be at my sister's," she said tightly. "I'll get my things later."

"Come on, Dorry," Dave pleaded.

She ignored him and walked out. Dave leaned desolately against the wall. Pink, embarrassed, took a tentative step into the room.

"Hey, man, I'm sorry. I didn't know I was saying anything wrong."

"It's not your fault, Pink," said Handley. "It's mine," He grunted softly and held up his right fist. "I guess it's always been my fault." he added quietly, looking at his closed fist.

The day after Dora left him, Dave Handley began training. In exercise pants, sweatshirt, and ring shoes, he worked out in a corner of the Midwest Gym, with Pink helping him. As he was jumping rope that first day, there was some commotion at the front end of the gym. Dave and Pink looked over and saw a crowd gathering. A tall, smiling young black man had just come in, accompanied by two older white men. There was a sudden electricity in the gym: it was the arrival of Lester Jackson, the Pan American Games champion.

"Well, there he is," Pink said.

Hit and Run

"Yeah." Handley danced around a bit to keep warm. As he moved, he continued to watch the front of the gym. He studied Jackson: a wide, brilliant smile in a dark face; full head of neatly trimmed hair; an obviously expensive vested suit and sport shirt: everything first-class. There was a sad envy in Dave Handley's face as he watched the young man lead the crowd into the locker room.

Pink saw him watching and slapped him smartly on the shoulder. "Two hands, Davey, just like everybody else," he said matter-of-factly.

"Yeah. Two hands."

"The way I figure it," Pink said, "the kid is going to try to stick you to death. He's fast, so he'll hit and run, hit and run. What you got to do is cut off the ring on him, slow him down, and throw strong counter-punches, follow me? You can handle his hit-and-run tactics, Davey."

"Yeah, sure. I can handle him."

Resolutely, Handley resumed his workout.

At home that night, Handley was lying on the couch reading the latest issue of *The Ring*. On the floor beside him was a TV dinner tray and an empty milk glass. He had his stockinged feet propped up on the couch. On a table behind the couch, a small radio was playing softly. Presently a voice said, "The time at WGN-Chicago is 8:00 P.M. In a moment, WGN's News on the Hour—"

Handley reached over and turned off the radio. He tossed the magazine on the floor and rested his head back to stare up at the dirty gray ceiling. Unconsciously, he moved one hand to his mouth and began to chew his nails. Suddenly there was the sound of someone trying to unlock the apartment door. Handley's face lit up with anticipation. He quickly got up and hurried to the door. Jerking the door open, he found a black woman with a large bag of groceries.

"Will you just look at me, Mr. Handley!" she exclaimed. "Trying to get in the wrong apartment. Bet you thought it was your wife, didn't you?"

Handley forced a weak grin. "Yeah, I sure did, Mrs. Little. Here let me take that bag for you."

He carried the groceries down the hall for the woman and waited while she opened her own apartment door. Then he walked listlessly back to his own place. He stood in the middle of the room for a long moment, indecision etched on his face. Then, as he decided what he was going to do, his expression became set. He quickly put on his shoes, grabbed his ancient leather jacket, and left the apartment.

Outside, Dave jogged down the dark street and crossed to a cigar store that had an outside phone booth. He got out a dime, then had to search through a worn, cluttered wallet for a scrap of paper which had the number he wanted on it. He dialed the number. Presently there was an answer.

"Laverne? Yeah, this is Dave. Say, is Dorry there? Could I talk to her, please? What? Yeah, I know that, Laverne. Yeah, I know that too. Look, would you mind just asking her if she'll talk to me?"

He waited, looking slightly disgusted in the dim light of the booth. Folding the scrap of paper several time, he tapped it irritably on the ledge beneath the phone. Then his face brightened.

"Yeah, Dorry? Hi, honey. How are you? Me? I'm okay, I guess. Kind of lonesome. You know I don't like to stay by myself, Dor."

He looked down at the floor of the booth, listening. His expression was like that of a child, being chastised. After a moment, he spoke again.

"Dorry, I didn't mean to lie to you, honest. I was going to

work up to telling you, see, but all of a sudden you backed me into a corner, you know. I couldn't think of nothing else to do but say I didn't take the fight. What? No, I know that's no excuse, Dor. I ain't trying to make no excuses. What? What'd I call for? Well, I wanted to say I was sorry and—"

Again he listened, frowning.

"The fight? Sure, it's still on. But listen, Dorry, I seen this guy I'm fighting, and he don't really look all that tough. Even Pink says all's he's got is two hands. Huh?"

Now he listened for a long time: patiently at first, nodding in agreement at whatever his estranged wife was saying; then he shrugged a couple of times, as if helpless in the face of her verbal onslaught; and finally, he grew impatient with it all and began to tap restlessly with the folded scrap of paper again. When he spoke again, it was with a tone of resignation and defeat.

"All's I know, Dor, is that if you *wanted* to come back to me, you could. Nothing's holding you over there, except maybe Laverne, and we both know how she feels about me. What? No, I ain't saying nothing about your sister. Yeah, I know she's only looking out for your best interests. Yeah. Yeah. Okay. Sure—"

His voice trailed off until finally he was simply nodding at the receiver. Then he leaned forward and put his head against the glass of the booth. He stood like that for a moment, a picture of frustration. When it became obvious that there was no longer a voice at the other end of the line, he slowly hung up the phone.

Stepping out of the booth, he zipped his jacket up to the throat, shoved his hands into its pockets, and walked like a whipped dog down the dark and lonely side street.

In the gym, Dave Handley began working like a man possessed. The speed bag. Heavy bag. Medicine ball. Sit-ups.

The rope. He wore a sweatshirt under a tee shirt under a sleeveless jersey—and the perspiration of his workout made a dark, wet spot through all three. Gradually his weight dropped: 208 down to 204, down to 201, down to 198. He began to harden.

Pink was constantly with him: holding a wet sponge to douse him, keeping time when he sparred, rubbing his upper arms to keep the muscles loose. When Pink thought he had worked out enough, he would say, "Come on, Davey, knock off. You keep up this pace, you'll kill yourself."

But Handley would shake his head: no. He kept at it: working, working, working. Hangers-on in the gym began to notice him. Other fighters commented that they had never seen him work so hard. It worried Pink.

"Dave, ain't you afraid you'll peak out? Get your edge too soon?"

Handley shook his head. "It's okay, Pink. It's okay. I ain't trained in a long time. Feels good, man. Feels good."

He worked every day until Lester Jackson came in to train. Then, while the young gold medal winner hung up his tailored suit and silk shirt, put on his new training leather and new satin, Dave, over in a corner of the locker room, stripped off his faded cottons and old, scuffed protector harness, and got out his plain corduroy trousers and flannel shirt to put on after he showered. He and Jackson took note of each other every day, but they did not speak. As the days passed, Handley grew noticeably quieter and more subdued.

While working out one morning, Handley was tapped on the shoulder by Pink, who bobbed his chin toward the front of the gym. An older man had just entered: about 60, impeccably tailored in a fine cashmere topcoat and beaver fedora. He was Mr. Jake, the czar of illegal gambling on the West

Side. Accompanying him was a man about Handley's age, with a countenance as tough as Handley's but without the scar tissue; also nicely dressed, with an air of hard confidence about him. His name was Eddie.

"Ain't that your pal from the old neighborhood?" Pink asked.

"Eddie, yeah," Handley answered.

"I see he's still a strong-arm for Mr. Jake."

Handley shrugged. "Yeah, well, it pays good, I guess."

"You gonna say hello to him?"

"Aw, I don't think so. We ain't seen each other in a while. Besides, when he's with the man, he's like working, you know?"

Pink nodded and watched Mr. Jake and Eddie walk back to Leo Marvel's office.

In his office, Leo Marvel was looking at a freshly-printed fight poster. It was black-and-red on white stock, and read:

CHICAGO STADIUM
OCTOBER 23   8:30 P. M.
MARVEL ENTERPRISES PRESENTS
30 ROUNDS OF BOXING
MAIN EVENT—HEAVYWEIGHTS
CHARLEY NEAL VS. WILLIE EDWARDS
10 ROUNDS
SPECIAL BOUT
LESTER JACKSON
PAN AMERICAN GAMES CHAMPION
PRO DEBUT
VS.
DAVE HANDLEY
FORMER C0NTENDER
6 ROUNDS

"Very nice, Leo," said Mr. Jake, noting the poster as he entered the office.

"Oh, Mr. Jake," Leo said anxiously, jumping up. "I didn't see you come in. Here, take my chair, please."

"Thank you, Leo," said the older man. He sat behind the desk while Leo took one of the wooden chairs. Eddie stood idly by the door; Leo could feel him at his back.

Mr. Jake put on a pair of silver-rimmed glasses and studied the poster more closely. His concentration was disturbed by a *meow* from the mother cat in her box of kittens in the corner. Mr. Jake glanced distastefully at the box but said nothing. Leo swallowed dryly as the gambler continued to peruse the poster.

"Yes, very nice, indeed, Leo," Mr. Jake said at last. "You're coming along quite well as a promoter. Seems like only yesterday you were scratching together four-round club fights. Now—" he waved an all-encompassing hand, "—your own gym, your own office, and *thirty* rounds of boxing at the Stadium. Impressive, Leo. Most impressive."

Leo shrugged modestly. "I've been lucky, Mr. Jake." His expression begged: *What do you want?*

"No, you've been smart, Leo. You've used your head. This, for instance," he tapped his glasses case on the poster. "This bum Handley you picked to test young Jackson. I'm sure you gave the matter a lot of thought before selecting him. Am I right?"

"Well, yeah, I guess so—"

"I *know* so, Leo—because I know you. And I know you would have figured that there's a lot of heavy money behind this Jackson kid. Not just Chicago money, but Detroit money, New York money, Miami money—money from all over. Money that wants to see this boy go all the way up to a title shot within three years. That sort of thing is good for our particular economy; it stimulates people to bet. You understand what I'm saying?"

"You're saying you, uh, don't want him to lose."

"Exactly."

Leo relaxed a little. "Nothing to worry about, Mr. Jake. Handley couldn't whip this kid with a friend. See, Handley's a pushover for a scientific left—"

"Please," Mr. Jake said, raising a hand, "no lectures on the sport. What I want from you is a simple yes or no. The story I hear is that this Handley is training like this was a title go. People who know say they ain't seen nobody train like him since Billy Conn. Now tell me, Leo: is there even an outside chance that this bum can whip Lester Jackson?"

"Absolutely not," Leo said, shaking his head emphatically.

"Guaranteed?"

Leo swallowed dryly again. "Guaranteed," he said, forcing the word out.

"Fine, Leo, fine," the dapper gambler said with a smile. "Your word is good enough for me." He rose and came around the desk. The mother cat jumped out of her box and brushed against his leg. Brutally, Mr. Jake kicked the cat against the wall. It screeched in pain and ran back to its box. "You shouldn't keep cats around, Leo," Mr. Jake lectured. "They get hair all over your clothes."

Leo said nothing. Eddie opened the door for Mr. Jake and followed him out of the office. When they were gone, Leo hurried to the cat and gently examined it. There was nothing broken. He sat down next to the box and took the cat onto his lap. As he petted and comforted it, he glared hatefully at the still open office door and blinked back tears of frustration at what a man sometimes had to take to get ahead in the world.

Out in the gym, Mr. Jake paused and looked at Dave

Handley. The fighter was working the speed bag, his heels rising and falling with the steady, even tempo of his punches. Mr. Jake studied him for a moment, then turned to Eddie. "This bum is the guy you knew from before, right?"

"Yes, sir. We grew up in the same neighborhood."

"I think maybe I'll let you have a talk with him."

"Yes, sir. What kind of talk?"

"Friendly. Like a couple of guys who ain't seen each other for a while. See what *he* thinks his chances are. See, Eddie, once a guy gets to *thinking* he can win, then he's got a chance. Know what I'm saying?"

"Yes, sir."

"Maybe I've got nothing to worry about, I don't know. But I just ain't a hundred percent sure of Leo. Anybody that's a sucker for cats might be a sucker for bums like Handley, too. So you find out for me, huh, Eddie?"

"Yes, sir, Mr. Jake, I will."

Later that day, after he finished training, Handley was walking home to his apartment. He passed the phone booth he had used to call Dora. His pace slowed and he glanced at the booth. Indecision was etched in his face again; he wanted to call her, but he was reluctant to because he was afraid it would be futile. Finally he forced himself away from the temptation of the booth and continued on his way. As he was about to cross the street, he heard a voice calling him.

"Hey, Davey! Davey, wait up!"

Turning, he saw Eddie trotting up the sidewalk toward him. He remained on the curb, waiting for him.

"Hey, you old palooka, how you been?" Eddie asked, running up. "I seen you in the gym today. I wanted to say hello but I was with the old man, you know?"

Dave shrugged. "Yeah, sure."

Hit and Run

"Hey, come on around the corner to Minocci's; let's split a pizza."

"I better not, Ed. I'm in training."

"Hey, one pizza ain't gonna kill you," Eddie said. He took Dave's arm and pulled him toward the corner. "Come on, we'll get a low-cal pizza; have Minocci leave off some of the sauce. Come on—"

Dave thought about the empty apartment waiting for him. He finally allowed himself to be pulled around the corner. Half an hour later, they were facing each other in a booth with a big pizza on a tray between them. Eddie had a pitcher of beer on his side of the table; Dave had water. The two men were reminiscing.

"Hey, you remember back in '59 when we was twelve years old?" Eddie said. "We tried to sneak through the gate at the Stadium to see Sonny Liston box Nino Valdes? We kept waiting and waiting for the gatekeeper to look the other way, and when he finally did and we got inside, the fight was all over. Liston knocked him out in the third."

"Yeah," Handley grinned around a mouthful of pizza. Talking while he chewed, he said, "Remember those three fights Jimmy Bozeman had with Harold Brooks? In the first he lost a ten-round split decision, in the second he lost a ten-round *unanimous* decision, and in the third fight he was knocked out in the fifth. Remember that fat guy at ringside that yelled into the ring, 'You better quit fighting this guy, Bozeman! There ain't nothing left but death!' Remember that?"

"Yeah, yeah," said Eddie, trying to keep from choking with laughter. For a few minutes, he really enjoyed Handley's company, enjoyed talking over old times, remembering days when life was not nearly so complicated. He sighed wistfully. "Man, there was some fine heavyweights back in those days.

Remember Mike DeJohn?"

"Yeah. And Eddie Machen."

"Yeah. And Charley Norkus."

"Good fighters, all of 'em," said Handley.

"Man, they don't make 'em like they used to, huh, Davey?"

"No. Not no more."

Eddie took a swallow of beer and remembered what he was there for. "We sure had some times crashing the gate at the Stadium, though. And now look at us: I get complimentary ringside seats from Mr. Jake, and you go in the fighters' door. We still don't pay." He pursed his lips in thought for a moment. "Jeez, who'd ever have thought my old pal Davey woulda turned out to be a fighter."

"Yeah, well, life's funny." A flash of Dora passed through his mind. And sometimes not so funny, he thought.

Eddie's expression turned sly. "So, what do you think about this kid Jackson, Dave? You think you can handle him?"

"I'm gonna try."

"Word's around that you're training like it was a title go."

"I'm getting in shape, yeah."

"You really think you can take him?"

Dave leaned forward on his forearms and lowered his voice confidentially. "I think I have a very good chance here, Eddie. Very good. Jackson's gonna use a hit-and-run style against me, see; all's I have to do is cut off the ring on him and get in my licks. I'm looking to go the distance and get the decision."

Eddie nodded thoughtfully. "Well, I'll be there at ringside yelling for you, pal." Eddie smiled as he spoke, but his eyes turned very hard.

When he left Eddie and started home again, Dave passed

the same phone booth for the second time. On impulse, he stopped and called Dora's sister's house.

"Hello, Laverne? Can I please speak with Dorry?"

He waited. After a moment, Laverne returned to the line. Dave's expression, as he listened to her words, was one of hurt.

"You mean she won't talk to me at all? Not even to say hello? What? No, I didn't call up to argue. I just wanted to see how she was, is all. Okay, so she's just fine. I don't see why she can't tell me herself."

Dave looked down dejectedly as he listened to Laverne's response. He blinked his eyes several times and wiped his nose on the cuff of his jacket sleeve. His face turned sad, helpless.

"Okay," he said finally, his voice low, almost listless. "Okay, I get the message."

After he hung up, he stood there in the booth for a long time.

The next afternoon, when Dave finished his roadwork in the park and jogged up to the gym entrance, a man in a business suit was standing there. "Mr. David Handley?" he asked.

"Yeah, that's me."

The man handed him a summons. "Divorce papers, Mr. Handley. Sorry to have to do this to you so close to the fight. Good luck against Jackson."

"Yeah, thanks." Dave watched him walk away, then stared at the summons he was holding. After a moment, he shook his head resignedly and went on into the lobby of the athletic club. At the cigar counter he bought a packaged sandwich, a carton of milk, and two apples. Then he went outside and crossed the street into Garfield Park again. He sat on a bench in the warm afternoon sun and began eating.

As he ate, Dave took the divorce summons out of his pocket and tried to read it. He frowned; it was too legal, too complex. Finally, he shrugged and stuffed it back into his jacket pocket. He finished the sandwich and the milk, and stuffed the sandwich paper into the empty carton. As he was doing that, he glanced up and saw Lester Jackson coming into the park. The young black man walked to a nearby bench and sat down, stretching his long legs out in front of him. Knowing that Jackson could not help seeing him, Handley took the paper-stuffed carton and lobbed it toward a trash barrel twenty feet away. He sunk it, dead center. Grinning, he looked over at Jackson. The young fighter grinned back and held up two fingers: two points for a basket.

Dave reached into his paper bag and took out the two apples. He looked over at Jackson again. "Want an apple?" he asked.

"Don't mind if I do," said Lester. He came over and sat down on the bench with Handley, who handed him one of the apples. "Couple of times in the gym I was gonna pass the time of day with you," Jackson said, "but my manager said not to."

Dave nodded. "Gotta listen to your manager," he allowed.

"Yeah, he say it ain't good to get friendly with one's opponents."

"He's got a point, I guess," said Dave.

The two men sat looking straight ahead, munching on their apples. There were city sounds around them, but they were in their own little vacuum.

"My manager, he say you been fighting for a while," Jackson commented.

"About fourteen years," said Dave.

Jackson laughed and shook his head. "Man! Fourteen years ago, I wudn't but six years old!"

Dave smiled. "Yeah, Muhammad Ali had just defended the title for the ninth time when I started fighting. Knocked out Zora Folley in the seventh. Right after that he had all that trouble with the draft and quit fighting. The heavyweight title was wide open. Every young fighter around dreamed of getting a shot at it." Dave grunted softly. "You know, since I've been born, there's been eleven heavyweight champions. Some people count how many Presidents there's been; but me, I count up the heavyweight champions."

"Hey, I know what you mean, man," Jackson said. "The heavyweight title: that's where it's at."

"Yeah. The pot of gold at the end of the rainbow. It's always out there, waiting for somebody to come and take it." He turned and looked steadily at Jackson. "But it ain't easy to get, you know. There's lots of guys like me that a man's gotta get past first. Guys like me, we're called 'trial horses'; we're the backbone of the fight game; we weed out the ones that shouldn't have the title. You know what I mean?"

Jackson nodded slowly. "What you saying is that nobody gets a free ride, right?"

"Right. Not with me, leastways."

"Tha's the way it ought to be," Jackson declared. "I know I wouldn't want it to be no different. I plan to go all the way to that title, and I want the road to be as tough as it can be. That way, when I do get up there, I'll appreciate what I got."

Dave grinned at him. "You're a pretty smart kid," he said. "Listen, are you in shape for me? Good shape?"

Jackson smiled a lazy smile. "I'm in shape for *anybody*," he said easily.

"Reason I ask is because personally I am *ready*. I mean, man, I'm going in there to fight."

"I'm glad to hear it, man," Jackson replied. "Cause I want to look *good* for all the peoples gonna be watching me, see? I wouldn't look good if you didn't put up a fight."

"I don't think you get my full meaning," Dave said quietly. "What I'm saying is, I think I can win."

Jackson frowned slightly and looked curiously at Handley. "You serious? You think you can beat me?"

"You bet."

"All right!" Jackson said, delighted. He grinned happily. "Hey, you know I was kinda afraid they was gonna give me a bum to begin with; a guy that would just make me look good, you know?"

Dave shook his head vigorously. "Not me, kid. I ain't no tanker, never will be."

"Well, that is *fine*, my friend! You and me, we'll give the turkeys a fight." Lester held his hand out, palm up, for some skin; instead, Dave shook his hand in the conventional way. Lester beamed. "Okay, tha's cool. You all right, Big Dave." He rose to leave. "Hey, thanks for the apple."

Dave shrugged off the thanks. "See you at the fight, kid."

Across the street, in the deserted locker room of the gym, Eddie cornered Pink. "Mr. Jake has got a job for you, pal," the hoodlum said.

"I got a job," Pink replied sullenly.

Eddie's lip curled and he kicked Pink hard in the ankle. Pink groaned and dropped to a bench, clutching his ankle.

"Let's start all over, dummy," Eddie said in a quiet, hard voice. "Mr. Jake has got a job for you."

"Okay, okay," Pink groaned. "What is it?"

Eddie sat down beside him. "Mr. Jake and some other gentlemen who are interested in Lester Jackson's future think maybe Big Dave Handley might have trained too hard for this fight. They're worried that he might beat Jackson."

Pink shook his head. "I been watching Jackson train.

Hit and Run

Dave ain't got a chance."

Eddie put a stiff finger an inch from Pink's nose. "You want to guarantee that with your life?"

Pink shifted his eyes, frightened. "No."

"Then shut up and listen. You know how Dave always likes to suck on a couple of oranges before a fight?"

"Yeah," Pink reluctantly admitted.

"You're the one that's going to bring him the oranges, right?"

Pink did not answer. Eddie jabbed the stiff forefinger against his chest.

"Right?" he insisted on an answer.

"Yeah, right," Pink said.

"Okay. On fight night you'll get the oranges from me."

"You might as well pull out your cannon and blow me up right now," Pink said defiantly, " 'cause I ain't going to do nothing to hurt Dave!"

"Who's asking you to?" Eddie said innocently. "You think I'd hurt Dave? He's my friend too, you know."

"Then what's this business about the oranges?"

"They'll be doped, but with just enough stuff to slow him down; just enough so's his reflexes won't be as sharp."

"That's wonderful," said Pink. "Then Jackson can rip his head off."

"Jackson's manager will be in on it," Eddie lied. "He'll keep his boy in check. The kid will coast to a nice six-round decision. Everything'll be clean, no knockouts, no blood."

"I don't know," Pink said reluctantly.

"Look," Eddie told him coldly. "I'm not exactly making a request here. What I'm doing is giving you the message from Mr. Jake. If you don't like the deal, he'll just have you put in the hospital and we'll find somebody new to work Handley's corner. In the end it still comes out like Mr. Jake wants it."

Pink stared down at the floor, his expression helpless and forlorn. He knew that he was boxed in: what Eddie had just told him was true; there was no way out for him. Shaking his head at the injustice of it all, Pink buried his face in his hands. Eddie sneered at the trainer's display of emotion.

"I'll meet you outside Gate Ten a half-hour before the fight," he told Pink.

Eddie left the locker room and went down to the lobby. He called Mr. Jake from a phone booth.

"It's all arranged, sir. I'll give him the oranges just before the fight. I laid a line on him about Jackson's manager being in on it. Promised that the kid would carry Handley to a six-round decision. Him and Handley are *both* going to be in for a surprise after Handley eats that doped orange. Jackson will rip his head off."

"That's very good, Eddie," said Mr. Jake. "Listen, make sure that orange is doped good. I'm going to lay a bundle out of town that Handley will be stopped in one round."

"No problem, Mr. Jake," Eddie promised.

On the day before the fight, when Dave finished his last workout and walked back to the locker room, all the other fighters in the gym stopped their workouts and followed him. There were about a dozen of them, all sizes, weights, and colors, most of them preliminary fighters like Handley, who made their precarious living in four- and six-rounders. They eased quietly into the locker room and watched as Dave stripped off his sweatshirt, tossed it on a bench, and opened his locker door. They saw Dave's mouth drop open; he stared incredulously into the locker. Hanging inside was a new satin robe, red and white, with his name across the back; and a pair of matching satin trunks with his initials on one leg.

"Hey, Pink, where'd this stuff come from—?" he asked,

turning. Then he saw the other fighters. They smiled in unison, and a couple of them raised clenched fists. A tough veteran middleweight named Teddy Falcon stepped forward.

"We all chipped in for it, Davey," he said. "We figure you're one of us, you know. You could have just made a show of fighting this Jackson kid, but you been going at it like there was a title on the line. You're gonna show 'em that you ain't no bum. You're gonna look good in there tomorrow night. And win or lose, when you look good, we all look good—'cause you're one of us. The robe and trunks are just our way of saying good luck."

They did not wait for Dave to thank them. He watched with a dry mouth as they all filed out, leaving him alone. Then he took the robe and tried it on. It had been a long time since he had owned a satin robe. Walking over to look at himself in the mirror over the lavatories, his mind went back to the early days when he had been undefeated, with 12 straight wins, and there had been talk of putting him in against Jerry Quarry or Jimmy Ellis or some other name contender. Then another up-and-coming kid had knocked him out and his stock had dropped drastically. From then on it had been win a few, lose one, win a few, lose one, until now he was 42 and 18, and a six-rounder a few times a year was all he could look forward to. Sighing, looking at himself in the mirror, he wished he had learned a trade of some kind, or at least finished high school. Maybe Dorry was right, he thought: maybe an over-the-hill fighter *was* nothing but a bum.

He shook his head. No, bums don't wear satin. Tomorrow night he would show the world he was no bum!

He went back to his locker to hang up his new robe so it would look nice for the fight. In case Dorry decided to watch.

On Saturday night before the fight, Eddie stopped in the

office of a doctor who owed Mr. Jake several favors. He opened a paper bag and poured half a dozen fresh oranges onto the counter in the doctor's examination room. "Take your pick, Doc," he said.

The doctor squeezed several of the oranges and selected one. Removing a cloth from a tray, he picked up a hypodermic needle, tested it for flow and in a quick, deft movement injected the chosen orange with the contents of the vial.

"Don't get it mixed up with the others," he told Eddie.

"Don't worry," Eddie answered. He took a roll of adhesive tape from his pocket, tore off a one-inch strip, and affixed it to the doped orange. "Thanks, Doc," he said.

Outside Gate Ten at the stadium, Eddie waited with the bag of oranges until a somber-looking Pink shuffled up to him. Eddie handed Pink the bag. "It's the one with the adhesive tape stuck to it."

"You sure it won't hurt him?"

"Not a chance. All's it's going to do is slow him down."

Pink sighed quietly and took the bag. He started to walk away.

"Don't forget," Eddie reminded him, "this is for Mr. Jake. If you let him down, he'll be very unhappy. Very."

"Sure, sure," Pink mumbled to himself, going on his way.

"I'll stop by the dressing room later to see if everything is okay," Eddie hollered after him.

At seven o'clock, when Handley arrived at his section of the big dressing room, Pink was there waiting for him. Handley saw the brown bag on the bench. "Those my oranges?"

"Yeah."

"Peel me one, will you, while I change."

"Sure." Pink opened the bag. With his back to Handley he removed the orange with the tape on it and studied it for a moment; then put it back and took out a good orange.

Hit and Run

Handley stripped down and strapped on his leather protector. Then he slipped into his new trunks and sat down to put on his socks. Pink handed him the peeled section of orange. Handley tossed one in his mouth, sucked all the juice out of it and threw the pulp into a trash container.

"Jackson is going to get the surprise of his life, Pink," he said. He tossed another orange section into his mouth.

Pink frowned thoughtfully. "You really think you can take this kid, Dave?" he asked.

"You seen how I been training, Pink. I'm *ready*. I can get around his hit-and-run style. I think I'll go the distance with him, and I think I'll get a decision."

"Jeez," Pink said quietly, "wouldn't that be something?"

Dave finished the last of the orange sections. "Let me have another one, Pink."

"Sure." Once again Pink put the doped orange aside and peeled a good one for Handley. After he gave the sections to Dave, he peeled the doped orange and deliberately began eating it himself.

A few minutes later, Eddie came into the dressing room. "Hey, Big Dave, how you feeling?"

"Good, Eddie. I feel good."

"Great. I just dropped in to wish you luck."

"Thanks, Eddie."

As Handley laced up his ring shoes, Eddie looked around their corner. On the end of the bench he saw a small pile of orange peels. In the pile was the peel with the adhesive tape on it. Eddie winked at Pink. The trainer nodded.

After Eddie left, Dave bobbed his chin at the door and said, "Eddie's a pretty nice guy, you know."

"Salt of the earth," Pink replied.

Just then Leo Marvel stuck his head in the door. "Okay, Handley, you're up. Get in the ring."

★ ★ ★ ★ ★

At last it was time. Under the bright ring lights, the fighters were introduced and called to the center of the ring for their instructions. When that formality was over, they returned to their corners and waited for the bell.

Round One.

Dave Handley came out of the corner with everything he had learned in 14 years of ring warfare—plus the conditioning that had resulted from the hardest physical training he had ever done. All of it showed: he was at once at his best against the young Pan Am Games champion.

Lester Jackson was smooth, stylish, with fast hands and fast feet. He moved and stuck and jabbed like a young Ali or a modern-day Ray Robinson. His speed and concentration were flawless. But none of it worked against Handley in that first round.

When Jackson flicked his left jab, it landed not on Handley's face but on his glove. When he threw his overhand right, more often than not it missed completely. When he danced around the ring, Handley did not chase him; instead he stepped to the side and cut off the ring on the younger man. All the while, Lester Jackson was smiling: when his jabs were short, when his hooks missed, when his footwork was neutralized—he smiled. But he was constantly on the defense as Handley, head tucked behind his cocked right, methodically pressed forward, working him to the body trying to slow him down. Handley was confident, determined, professional. He moved forward steadily, building up points with a cautious but effective aggressiveness. When the bell sounded, Handley returned to his corner knowing he had won the first round.

"I can take this kid, Pink!" he said eagerly. "I'm gonna win this fight!"

"Keep working him, Davey," Pink said. His words were slightly slurred. When he leaned over to wipe Handley's face, he dropped the sponge.

"What's the matter?" Dave asked. "You sick or something?"

"I'm okay," Pink said. He retrieved the sponge, rinsed it in the water bucket, and wiped Handley's face. Then he began to massage the fighter's shoulders.

"He's not as good as I thought he'd be, Pink," Handley said. It was nervous energy talking now, and the words kept coming. "He's not as fast as he looked in training. And his punches ain't sharp, you know; even when he lands, they don't bother me. I'm cutting off the ring on him pretty good, don't you think? I mean, his footwork is okay, but if I keep cutting the ring in half, it won't do him no good—"

The warning buzzer sounded for Round Two. As Pink started to step through the ropes onto the ring apron, he slipped and almost fell. Quickly he regained his balance.

"Pink, you sure you're okay?" a frowning Dave Handley asked.

"Yeah, yeah, fine," the drugged trainer replied. "Go out and work him this round, Big Dave."

"I'll work him, Pink," Handley said eagerly. "I'll work him for you, pal."

The bell rang. Handley moved out to the center of the ring and resumed his cautious forward attack. But this time Lester Jackson did not back up. Instead he stood flatfooted and began to tattoo Handley with a series of incredibly fast jabs and hooks. Handley was taken completely by surprise as the blows rained on him with a vengeance. Before he could recover his composure, Jackson finished his flurry and backed off.

Handley went after him. The young black began to move

around the ring again—so fast now that Handley was unable to cut him off. As Jackson moved, he flicked out a steady tempo of hard sharp lefts, each of them finding Handley's eye or cheekbone. Handley's head began to snap back with each blow. Trying to regain his earlier momentum, Dave rushed forward in a sudden attack. Jackson was ready for him. All but one of Handley's punches missed—and Jackson countered with half a dozen brutal combinations. Handley's knees buckled. He rushed forward again. Jackson drilled him with a solid right. Handley dropped to one knee.

His mouth open, staring incredulously at the crowd, Handley took the mandatory eight-count. As soon as he got back up, Lester Jackson was all over him again. The Lester Jackson of the second round was a far different fighter from the Lester Jackson who had allowed Handley's hopes to soar so high in the first round. This Lester Jackson was faster, smoother, harder hitting, and all business. He went after Handley with grim determination, landing with four or five remarkably accurate punches now for every awkward, missing blow that Handley attempted. Jackson's flashing gloves were like twin pistons: they turned Handley's face beet-red, bloodied his nose, cut his right eyebrow, knocked his mouthpiece out of the ring. Finally, from the sheer volume of blows hitting him, Handley went down again—all the way onto his back this time.

The noise of the crowd resounded in his head as he rolled over and began the long, unsteady climb back to his feet. The world around him was a fuzzy, slow-motion place, and from somewhere deep inside an echo chamber he could hear the referee's hollow toll: "—four! —five! —six!—"

Just at nine, Handley made it up again. He was a beaten man: it showed in his eyes. But he was not frightened, he did not retreat. He was not a tanker, he was not a bum. He stood his ground, knowing that he had only seconds left.

Jackson's final onslaught came: a series of half a dozen well-timed, well-placed punches that crashed squarely in Handley's battered face. They took the last ounce of fight out of him and he tumbled to the canvas for the third time.

Dave Handley's agony was over: a technical knockout in the second round.

In the dressing room, Handley was lying on a rubdown table, with Leo Marvel looking down at him. A doctor had just finished closing a cut over Handley's eye and sealing it with clips. When the doctor left, Leo said, "Can you sit up?"

"Yeah." The word came out slurred; Handley's sinuses were so swollen that he had to breathe through his mouth. "Where's Pink?" he asked as Leo helped him raise up and swing his feet over the side.

"I had one of the ushers take him to the gym. He was acting sick; said he thought he had food poisoning." Leo looked at Handley's abused face. "How do you feel?"

"Like I just lost a fight. Leo, that kid is *good!*"

"He's better than good. He'll have the title in three years."

"All that training," Handley said dismally. "And all I was good for was one fast round."

"That's the difference between being twenty and being thirty-four. But you put up a fight, pal. You didn't go in the tank. You didn't look like a bum. Incidentally, are you having trouble with your old lady?"

"Why?"

"Because some shyster divorce lawyer slapped a restraining order on me while you were in the ring. I got to hold up your purse."

Handley stared incredulously at Leo. "I can't believe Dora would do a thing like that."

"Believe it," Leo told him.

From the door, someone shouted, "Hey, Leo! They're ready to take pictures of you and Jackson now!"

"Okay!" Leo yelled back. "I gotta go now," he said to Handley. "Can you get dressed by yourself?"

"Yeah."

Leo started to walk away, then paused and turned back. "What are you gonna do now? Go back to the loading docks?"

Dave shrugged. "I guess. That's about all that's left."

Leo stared at him for a moment, then walked on out. Dave slipped off the table, steadied himself, and made his way slowly back to a row of shower stalls. He stepped into one of them still wearing his new trunks, and turned the water on full-force. With bowed head, he stood under the rushing water.

Back at the gym, in the locker room, Pink was sitting on a bench and Teddy Falcon was helping him drink some steaming coffee.

"You ain't kidding me, man," Falcon said. "You ain't got no food poisoning. You been doped, man. You know that?"

"I—know," Pink said thickly. "They—tried to—dope Dave—but I ate the orange—instead—"

"Who?" Falcon asked. "Who tried to dope him?"

"Mr.—Jake—"

From down the row of lockers came another voice. "Did I hear someone mention my name?"

It was Mr. Jake. With Eddie at his side.

"Shove off, Falcon," said Eddie. "And forget what you heard."

Teddy Falcon went out into the gym. There were a dozen other fighters sitting on the bleachers, crowded around a portable black-and-white TV, watching the rest of the Stadium

Hit and Run

card. "Hey, Teddy, come and see this, man," one of them said. "Charley Neal is killing Willie Edwards."

Falcon hurried over to the group.

In the locker room, Eddie had dragged Pink off the bench and was holding him up against a locker. He had an open switchblade held dangerously close to one of Pink's albino eyes.

"Do you have any idea how much money you cost me tonight?" Mr. Jake asked him coldly. "I had bets all over the country that Handley wouldn't last one round."

"You shouldn't gamble," Pink said with a silly grin.

Mr. Jake's expression turned livid. "Do it," he told Eddie.

But before Eddie could respond, Teddy Falcon hit him in the back of the head with a water bucket. Eddie dropped like a wet rope.

Falcon and the other fighters crowded around Mr. Jake. "Now wait a minute," Mr. Jake said. "Don't you guys know who I am?"

"You ain't nobody, man," said Falcon. "Not no more."

The dozen fighters engulfed the old gambler, knocking him onto one of the benches, raining practiced blows on every part of his body. They kept hitting him until he was dead.

Leo Marvel arrived back at the gym an hour later. Falcon told him what had happened. "We ain't sorry either," he affirmed. "It's tough enough trying to get along in this racket on the straight and narrow. Then guys like this Mr. Jake come along and try to make it even harder. It ain't right, Leo. We ain't sorry for what we done, even if we go to jail for it."

"Nobody's going to jail," Leo said quietly. He had two of the fighters get a wet sponge and bring Eddie around. "Listen to me, punk," he told the hood, "you were Mr. Jake's bodyguard and you let him get killed. Your reputation is gonna be zilch around this town when the word gets out. The way I figure it, you got maybe eight, ten hours to make tracks. If I was you, I'd go somewhere very far away, change my name, and get a job pumping gas or something. You know what I'm saying?"

Eddie, staring down at the still form of Mr. Jake, looked sick. He could only nod nervously in reply to Leo's advice.

"Okay, beat it," Leo said. "If you come back around, we'll all swear that *you* killed Mr. Jake."

After Eddie was gone, Falcon asked about Mr. Jake's body. Leo thought about it for a moment, then shrugged and said, "Take it downstairs and drag it down the alley. That's where guys like him belong."

While they were carrying Mr. Jake out, Leo went into his office to see how the kittens were doing.

It was a week after the body had been found that Sergeant Rubino, the homicide detective, came up to the gym to see Leo.

"Since this guy Jake is known to have had illegal gambling interests," Rubino said, "I thought you might know something about his death."

"Not me," Leo replied. "I'm a sports promoter. I don't have nothing to do with gamblers."

"From the condition of the body," Rubino said, "coroner figures he was either dragged down the alley by a car or stomped to death by a gorilla. He had bruises all over him."

"Well," Leo speculated, "a guy in his line of work probably had more enemies than friends."

"Yeah." The detective sighed wearily. "It sure would be a lot simpler if I could convince myself that it was a car instead of a beating. I could just close it out as another hit-and-run."

Hit and Run

Rubino looked across the gym at a figure hanging up speed bags. "Isn't that Dave Handley, the heavyweight?"

"Ex-heavyweight. He's retired. He works for me now. He's my gym manager."

"Good fighter, Handley. I always liked him. Lost five bucks on him against Jackson." Rubino lighted a cigarette. "I like the fights. Used to go all the time before I had a family. Can't afford it anymore, not on a cop's pay. Well, I won't keep you any longer, Mr. Marvel." He started to leave.

"How do you think this thing about Jake will turn out?" Leo asked, walking with him to the door.

Rubino shrugged. "I'll probably call it a hit-and-run. Simpler that way."

Leo nodded. "Listen, whenever you want to go to the fights, drop in and see me. I'll give you a couple of ringside passes."

"Terrific," Rubino said, smiling. "I got a friend that works for the coroner's office that I can take. He's a big fight fan too. Well, I better go. Got to write up that hit-and-run report."

After Rubino left, Leo went into his office and picked up the cat. Cradling her gently in one arm like a baby, he walked out to where Handley was working.

"Dave, I'm gonna take Queenie down to the vet to see if she needs vitamins," he said, a note of concern in his voice. "You keep an eye on the place while I'm gone."

"Sure, Leo," said Dave.

"Would you like some coffee, Mr. Louis?" a voice asked.

Dave looked around. It was Ethel, the nervous woman who was Leo's secretary. She was checking the top button of her blouse as she spoke.

"Yeah, I would, thanks," said Dave.

He was going to have to tell her his name was not Joe Louis.

When, in 1845, Henry David Thoreau built himself a crude house on remote Walden Pond and went to live there alone for two years, his stated purpose was to meditate on the hidden meaning of man's existence. Before long, however, the sounds of birds and animals in the woods had created an intense curiosity about the forest life that surrounded him, and soon his main interest had become the relationship between man and nature. Eventually he became the sole human in an environment of owls, squirrels, loons, fish, a variety of migratory birds, and many other living creatures. It was, for a time, a splendid life.

In the story that follows, another man seeks refuge and solitude in the woods, and also establishes a relationship with the wild things around him. Unlike Thoreau, however, he is not free to return to his former life. Not even when a strange woman reminds him of what he left behind . . .

Wild Things

Tree O'Hara lay prone on the ground and peered down at a little crossroads settlement through twelve-power binoculars. He was in a stand of tall pines six hundred yards or so up the mountain. The settlement, which did not even have a name, consisted of a Conoco gas station, a general store, and a roadhouse restaurant, each occupying a corner where the two mountain highways intersected. The fourth corner was unimproved and stood vacant except for a road sign which read: BUTTE 112.

It was Sunday afternoon and both the Conoco station and the general store were closed. The roadhouse restaurant was open but there was only one car parked in front of it: a five-year-old Cadillac with California plates.

Tree lowered the binoculars and got to his feet. He was a tall, once lean man, now beginning to flesh out with his age approaching forty; but still muscular, still quick. His most striking feature was his eyes; they were cold, and so black and flat they could have passed as sightless. He wore denim jeans and a Levi jacket over a faded work shirt; on his feet were lace-up lumberjack boots.

Leaving the edge of the pines, Tree walked briskly another hundred yards into the forest where he had left his horse. It was an Appaloosa, the horse: its foreparts white as a perfect cloud, its loin and shank spotted with round black markings. A mare, she stood just under fifteen hands high. When Tree had caught her, wild, in the Nez Perce National Forest four years earlier, she had been a fast and trim thousand or so pounds. Now he reckoned she weighed around twelve hundred. She had fattened out from their inactive life in the upper forest. Tree rode her on a regular basis only twice a month, when he came down to the settlement for supplies. But she was a happy animal, she loved the man who had captured her, and Tree guessed that if he ever had to do any hard riding, she would run her heart out for him.

The mare snorted and dug at the ground with one hoof as Tree approached. "Easy, Elk," he said quietly. Elk City, west of the Bitterroot Range, was where he had roped her, so he had named her 'Elk.' He rubbed her throat now to calm her, then stepped back to the saddle and put his binoculars in a case hanging from the horn. From a blanket roll behind the saddle he removed a pair of telephone-pole climbers and buckled them to the inside of his legs. From one saddlebag, he took a telephone lineman's intercept set—a receiver with a dial built into it and two magnesium clips for tapping into a wire—and hooked it onto his belt. "Keep still," he said to Elk, rubbing her throat again.

Walking fifty feet to a string of telephone poles that went up and over the mountain, Tree put on gloves and climbed one of them to its cross-beam. He hooked one arm around the beam to steady himself. With his free hand he laid the intercept set on the beam, attached the magnesium clips to one of the telephone wires, and got dial tone in the receiver. He dialed the number of the restaurant at the crossroads. John Grey Sky, the Shoshone owner, answered.

"John," said Tree without preliminary, "who's the Caddy belong to?"

"Oh, Tree, it's you. The Caddy? Nobody, man. A couple of sharpies and some bimbo passing through. They're slopping down beer and arguing about which route to take to Chicago."

"What do they look like?" Tree asked. "The men, I mean."

"Losers," said John. "Small-timers. Punks."

"You're sure? They're not just pulling an act?"

"Listen, brother, I know rabble when I see it," John assured him. "You're safe. Come on down. I got your supplies."

"Okay," Tree said. He had hesitated just a beat before answering. He hoped John Grey Sky had not noticed. He and John had been friends for twenty-five years, since attending Caribou Indian School together as young boys. It would never do to insult a friend of such long standing by doubting his judgment. If Grey Sky said he would be safe, Tree had to assume he would be. All the same, when he got back to Elk and put his equipment away, he took a loaded forty-five automatic from the saddlebag, jacked a round into the chamber, thumbed the safety on, and stuck it in his waistband under the Levi jacket where it could not be seen.

Tree led the Appaloosa to the edge of the pines and tied

her reins to a buffalobur shrub. The bush had just enough prickly spines on it to discourage Elk from nibbling the reins untied and following him, as she liked to do. "Be a good girl," he said, scratching her ears. "I'll bring you an apple."

Tree made his way down the slope and came onto the highway around the bend from the roadhouse. He approached the crossroads from behind the closed Conoco station, aware with every step of the gun in his waistband. From the side of the station he studied the car with the California plates. The tires were fairly worn, there was some rust on the chrome, and a small dent in the right rear fender had been left unrepaired. It looked like a loser's car, all right, just as Grey Sky had said. All the same, Tree was glad he had the gun.

Hurrying across to the rear of the roadhouse, Tree slipped through the open back door into the kitchen. John Grey Sky was scraping down his fry grill. "Hey, bro," he said.

"Hey, John." Tree's eyes swept the room, looking for anything out of the ordinary. Through the service window he could hear the voices of Grey Sky's three customers.

"Your supplies are there on the meat table," Grey Sky said.

Tree stepped over to a butcher block and examined the contents of a burlap bag: cheese, coffee, tins of meat, dry cereal, powered milk, beef jerky, magazines, a dozen fresh apples for Elk. "You get my animal food?" he asked the roadhouse owner.

"Under the table."

Tree pulled out a twenty-pound sack of processed dry animal food pellets. Similar to the food sold commercially to feed dogs and cats, it differed in that it contained flavors attractive to wild as opposed to domestic animals.

"You must be feeding half the wild things on that mountain," Grey Sky commented. "They're going to have to learn to scavenge all over again after you're gone."

Tree felt himself tense. "After I'm gone where?"

John Grey Sky shrugged. "Wherever."

Tree stared at his friend's back. Grey Sky could get a lot of money for betraying Tree O'Hara. Tree wondered if his friend was ever tempted.

The voices from the front of the restaurant grew louder. "You're getting a free lift to Chicago," a man's voice said. "Least you could do is be a little more friendly."

"Drop dead," a woman's throaty voice replied. There was a loud cracking noise then: the unmistakable sound of a face being slapped.

Frowning at each other, Tree and Grey Sky walked out from the kitchen. One of the men was standing, half bent over the table. The woman, seated, was staring up at him defiantly, one side of her face turning an angry red. "You kick dogs too?" she asked.

He hit her again, backhanded, on the other side of her face.

"Hey, man, no rough stuff in here!" Grey Sky said.

The man raised his hand again,

"Don't do it," Tree said. His voice, like his eyes, was flat and hard. It was clearly an order.

The man at the table turned around, one hand reaching for an empty beer bottle. "Who the hell are you?"

"Don't matter who I am," Tree said. He pulled back one side of his Levi jacket to expose the gun. "Don't hit her again."

"You gonna kill me if I do?" the man challenged with a sneer.

"No, just cripple you," Tree replied matter-of-factly. "I'll put one in your left instep. Blow your foot all to pieces."

The other man at the table intervened. "Hold it, chief," he said with a forced smile. "We don't want no hassle." He took the bottle from his friend's hand and put it down. "Come on, Lou, forget it. It's their patch." Picking up the check Grey Sky had given them, he looked at it and put some money on the table. "You coming?" he asked the woman.

"Not on your life," she said. Both sides of her face were now violently red.

"Please yourself. Come on, Lou."

The two men started to leave.

"Wait a minute, I've got a suitcase in that car!" the woman said urgently.

"Come on," Tree said. He went outside and stood with her while Lou opened the trunk and set her suitcase on the ground. The two men got in the Caddy and drove off.

The woman picked up her suitcase and followed Tree back inside. "Thanks," she said.

"Forget it," Tree told her. He studied her for a moment. She was, he guessed, an old twenty-five. There was no telling what her true hair color was; bottle blonde with black roots was what he could see. Too much makeup. A well-used but still good body. A bimbo, he thought. Like Grey Sky had said. The kind who'd take a free ride with two losers in a five year-old Caddy.

"What time's the next bus through here?" she asked, uncomfortable under Tree's scrutiny.

"Friday," said Grey Sky.

"*Friday!* This is only Sunday. Are you kidding me?"

"I never kid about anything as serious as bus service. Just once a week the bus comes over the mountain. Rest of the time it follows the Interstate around the mountain." Grey Sky looked over at his friend. Tree was staring at him, the realization having just dawned on him that the roadhouse owner was right. "Didn't think about that, did you, Galahad?" asked Grey Sky.

"Where the hell am I going to stay until Friday?" the woman asked in a half whine. "I don't have money for a motel."

"That works out just fine," Grey Sky said, " 'cause there's no motel anyway."

"Well, what am I gonna do!" she shrieked.

Tree looked at his friend. Grey Sky held both hands up, palms out.

"Not me, bro. I got my wife, four kids, my wife's mother, my unemployed brother-in-law and *his* wife and two kids—all in a two-bedroom, one-bath house. Sorry."

"Could you let her sleep here, put a cot in the kitchen—?"

Grey Sky shook his head. "My insurance don't allow overnight occupation of the premises. If she accidentally burned the place down, I couldn't collect a nickel. You're going to have to handle this good deed yourself, Galahad."

Tree glared at his friend. Grey Sky was obviously enjoying himself.

He could hear the woman panting as she trudged along behind him, lugging her suitcase with both hands. "How—much—farther—is it?" she gasped.

"Not far." Carrying the burlap bag of supplies on one shoulder, the sack of animal food on the other, Tree deliberately kept his pace slow to allow her to keep up with him. But when he saw that she was falling too far behind anyway, he stopped to let her rest.

"How come you live up in the mountains anyway?" she demanded. "You anti-social? Don't you like people?"

"As a matter of fact, I don't," he said, "very much."

Now it was her turn to study him. She was not sure

whether she liked what she saw. Those eyes of his didn't seem to have even a degree of warmth in them. "What'd that fellow down there say your name was? Galahad?"

"He was just trying to be funny. My name's Tree O'Hara."

"Tree? How'd you get a name like that?"

"My mother's family name. She was Indian. I'm one-quarter Minnetonka."

"Oh. Well, my name's Violet. I was named after a flower. You can call me Vi."

He nodded. "Come on," he said, "let's go on."

After one more rest stop, they came to the edge of the pines where Elk waited. As they approached, the mare snorted and pawed the ground edgily. "She smells you," Tree said. "She knows you're a woman. She's jealous. Come on, easy, baby," he said to Elk, putting an arm under her neck.

"Sure is a funny looking horse," Vi said. "Looks like the front of one and the back of another, stuck together."

Tree threw her an irritated glance. "This happens to be an Appaloosa. It's one of the most intelligent breeds of horse in the world, as well as one of the fastest. This horse has more stamina and endurance than any other breed you can name. It is the best stock horse, the best show horse—"

"All's I said was it was funny looking," she interrupted. "I'm sorry, but that's my opinion. Personally, I like Palaminos. Like Trigger, you know?"

Tree turned away in disgust. He felt as if he might be sick. *Trigger!* A Hollywood horse. Great spirits!

Tree lashed the two sacks one on top of the other just behind the blanket roll, then helped Vi into the saddle. She had to hike her skirt far up on her thighs in order to straddle the horse's back, but it did not seem to bother her. Tree noticed that her legs were well-rounded, fleshy; in fact, *all* of her was well-rounded and fleshy; she wasn't skinny anywhere, a fact that Tree approved of. He did not care for overly slim women; they always looked too fragile, like stickwood. Elk was of a different mind, however; the mare did not like the woman at all, and showed it by shuffling around skittishly and snorting loudly through flared nostrils. Tree finally had to cut up an apple and feed it to her so they could be on their way.

The trip to the cabin took another two hours, Tree leading the horse and rider while carrying Vi's suitcase in his free hand. He did not mind the walk; in fact, he was glad to get the exercise because he knew he was about ten pounds overweight. For the first couple of years after he had gone into hiding, he had made a point of exercising five days a week; calisthenics, weightlifting, jogging through the woods. That, along with chopping wood and pumping water out of his cistern, had kept him nicely in shape. But for the past three or four years he had grown lazy: sleeping late, not watching his diet, lying around like a much older man. He had become complacent in his mountain hideaway; he felt safe there; only rarely did he feel threatened anymore. After six years, he figured they had stopped looking for him.

Probably.

Maybe.

Tree and the woman arrived at the cabin just at twilight. It sat on a small clearing at the six-thousand-foot level, in the Beaverhead Forest, just east of the Continental Divide. When the clouds were high, Chief Joseph Pass could be seen from the porch; if they were very high, one could regularly see the moon and the sun at the same time, in different parts of the sky. The natural beauty of the place was indelible. The woman did not notice the scenery, however; she was too acutely aware of how isolated it was.

"Look, before we go in," Vi said, "I think we ought to get something straight. I had a falling-out with those other two guys because they had some weird ideas about how I should pay for my ride. I hope you're not thinking along those same lines as far as room-and-board goes."

"I'm not," Tree told her.

He said it a little too quickly to suit her. With a little too much determination. She hesitated on the porch, not following him into the cabin.

"Listen, no offense, you understand," she said, "but you're not—well, *peculiar* or anything, are you? I mean, living up here all alone—"

Tree returned to the doorway and faced her. "Why don't you lighten up?" he said. "You'll be safe here. But if you don't believe me, hike on back down the mountain and make other arrangements."

"A girl can't be too careful, is all I mean. I have this problem in that men usually find me very attractive—"

"I don't," Tree assured her. "My taste runs to darker women. When I get lonely, I ride down to the Salmon River Reservation. Lots of nice Nez Perce and Shoshone women down there. They like me because my skin's light. I stay for a few days and then come back home. I was just down to the reservation last week, so I'm settled for about a month now. Like I said, you're safe."

Turning, he walked away. When she finally came into the cabin several minutes later, she found her suitcase on the bed in the tiny bedroom. Tree had decided, he told her, to sleep on the couch. Not because he was such a gentleman; he just didn't like the idea of leaving her out in the main room alone all night. The main room—which was a kitchen-living-room combination—was where he had the television, short-wave receiver, his books, magazines, guns, ammunition: things he didn't want her fooling with. Sleeping on the couch, he could keep an eye on everything.

After Tree took care of Elk, rubbing her down briskly and putting her in the one-horse lean-to stable he had built onto the rear of the cabin, he came back into the cabin just in time to hear Vi, in the bedroom, say "Damn!"

"What's the trouble?" he asked.

"My cosmetics bag! It was in the back seat of the car! I don't have any makeup!"

"Tough break," he said indifferently.

He went into the kitchen, unpacked his supplies, and began preparing supper. Presently Vi came in to join him.

"Listen, I can cook," she said. "Really. Why don't you let me fix supper?"

"I'll do it," he replied. "I know how I like things."

Vi shrugged. Strolling, she looked the place over. "Got enough books," she commented. "All the comforts of home, too: radio, TV, everything. How do you manage it 'way up here?"

"I manage," was all he would tell her. He was not about to share any confidences with her. For electrical power he had illegally tapped into a main power line running across the mountain. For water he had a cistern next to the cabin. For television, a microwave dish which he had assembled on the roof, and which stole signals from the sky. For short-wave, a simple antenna wire strung up a high tree. For backup, a battery-operated generator, constantly charging off the tapped electricity.

"Okay if I look at these old magazines?" she asked, standing in front of the bookcase where he kept them.

"Sure. But do me a favor first. Step around back and make sure I closed the lean-to-door, will you? I don't want Elk to be in a draft."

While she was out of the cabin, he went quickly to the bookcase, took a small scrapbook from one of the shelves, and put it on top of the bookcase out of her sight and reach. Then he returned to the kitchen.

They shared an uneasy supper, both telling whatever lies they felt necessary to project or protect their respective images. Tree told Vi that he had originally come to live in the mountains to avoid the Vietnam draft, and had not gone back because he did not relish the idea of steady employment. He said he worked down at the roadhouse restaurant during tourist season to earn enough to live on the rest of the year. Vi told Tree that she was a model on her way to Chicago for a job at Marshall Field's. Because she was not due there for another week, she had accepted a ride with the two guys in the Cadillac. She had thought, she said, that they were legitimate businessmen, traveling salesmen or something, and had been very surprised to learn they were just a couple of petty hustlers.

Because each of them was lying, neither Tree nor the woman asked any questions of the other. They kept conversation to a minimum. After supper, Vi found that she was extremely tired. It was the climb and the altitude, Tree told her. "Your blood's thinned out. Better go to bed." She did, and fell into an immediate deep sleep.

When he was sure the woman was sleeping soundly, Tree slipped into the bedroom and got her purse. He brought it into the main room and searched it. There was an expired Illinois driver's license, a faded Social Security card, an address book containing no names that Tree recognized, an unmailed postcard with a photo on it of Harold's Club in Reno, and twelve dollars.

A loser's purse, for sure, Tree thought. He put it back in the bedroom.

Later, Tree fed Elk, opened his nightly bottle of beer,

chewed a little peyote, and watched an old John Garfield movie on some channel he was pulling in from a satellite. When the movie was over, he spread his sleeping bag on the couch, stripped, climbed in, and went to sleep, the .45 lying loaded and cocked on the floor just inches away.

The next morning, Vi found him out back of the cabin with his wild things. She stood out of sight around a corner of the cabin and watched him feed them from the sack of pellet food he had brought back. Vi was amazed at the number and variety of the animals. Some of them she could not even identify; others, like the rabbits, squirrels, and small deer she knew. Tree knelt right in their midst and fed them from his open hand. The sight of it was a wonder to her.

"You can come around and watch if you want to," he told her without looking around. "Just don't make any sudden moves."

Vi eased around the corner but stayed well back from the menagerie. "How'd you know I was there?" she asked curiously.

"This little mule deer told me," he said, scratching the middle forehead of a somewhat scroungy, unattractive deer. "I saw its nostrils flare; that meant a new scent was close by. Mule deer have very poor eyesight; they have to depend on their sense of smell for survival." He looked at her over his shoulder and grinned. "Plus which, I saw your shadow."

"Oh, you!" She moved a little closer. "What in the world are all of them? What's that reddish one with the yellow belly?"

"Ermine weasel. Turns pure white in the winter. That's when the trappers go after them."

"And that one, by the deer?"

"Pronghorn. It's a kind of bastard antelope." He stood up and started pointing. "That's a wolverine over there: baby

Wild Things

wolf. This big guy with the mark on his forehead is a badger. My mother's people named him. They called the white mark a 'badge.' Bet you didn't know 'badge' was an Indian word."

She shook her head. "No."

Tree smiled. "Most cops don't either."

"What's that one, with the partly webbed feet?"

"That's the one the ladies like: she's a mink. Next to her there, the big, shiny animal, that's a marten."

From a nearby limb came a clipped, scolding bird call. Tree looked over at a long-tailed black-and-white bird chattering noisily.

"All right," he said. He stepped out of the center of the wild things, closing the bag, and came to where Vi stood. From a wooden storage box, he removed another bag and scooped out a handful of its contents. "Bird seed," he said. He took her hand. It felt good. "Come on."

She let him lead her over to a low aspen and watched him hold out his open hand to feed the bird. "It's a magpie," he told her. "Biggest nag in the woods. Never gives you a minute's peace if he's hungry." After a couple of minutes, he closed his hand. "That's enough, Porky. I named him 'Porky' 'cause he's such a pig." He bobbed his chin toward another tree, a spruce. "Want to see an owl?" They walked over to a low, heavily-leafed limb where a small, unpleasant looking owl was hunched. It's oversized head seemed to comprise half of its body, and its big, direct eyes and hooked beak gave it a definite aura of hostility.

"Is it mad?" Vi asked, holding back tentatively.

"No," said Tree, "just sleepy. He'll burrow down into the leaves and go to sleep in a bit."

Tree fed the owl, as he had the magpie, from his palm. Then, with the last of the seed, he led Vi to a small, flat boulder jutting up from the ground like a fist. He sprinkled the rest of the seed on the flat of the rock and drew Vi a few feet away from it. "Now you'll see my favorite wild thing," he said quietly.

As they watched, a glossy black bird with wild yellow eyes swooped gracefully onto the rock and, after a cautious look around, began eating. As it ate, it honed its already razor-sharp talons on the rock.

"That's Midnight," Tree told her. "A raven."

"Won't it eat out of your hand like the others?"

"Not yet. He doesn't trust me enough yet. Someday he will. In another few years."

They walked back to the rear of the cabin. A few of the wild things were still there. Vi shook her head in wonder. "I didn't know animals were that friendly."

"They aren't, as a rule," Tree said. "That wolverine there, she's a natural enemy to the mink, the rabbit, and the marten. They're usually her prey. And the badger generally goes after the ermine weasel when he sees one. But they know I don't allow any fighting here in the clearing. I chase them off if they start fighting. It doesn't take long for them to learn that not fighting is best. Animals are a lot smarter than people."

"You really love them, don't you? These animals?"

"Yeah, I guess I do," Tree admitted. "It makes me feel good when I bring two natural enemies together and get them both to eat out of my hand at the same time."

"Too bad that can't be done with people," Vi remarked. "It would stop all the war and killing in the world."

"No, it wouldn't," Tree said quietly. "People would still kill, for sport. Man is the only animal that kills for sport. You'd never stop that. Man will always have to kill. It's his nature."

Vi stared at him. As he spoke, his eyes seemed to grow colder.

Wild Things

★ ★ ★ ★ ★

The next morning when Vi came out of the bedroom, Tree was at his short-wave set listening to an English-language broadcast from Moscow. "Don't look at me," she said. "I am totally out of makeup and I look *awful*."

Tree did look at her, and liked what he saw. "You look fine to me," he said. "Nice and scrubbed." He switched off the radio. "Want to go fishing with me?" he asked. He did not want to leave her alone in the cabin.

"I don't know how to fish."

"I'll teach you. Or you can just watch. We can take some food and have a picnic."

Vi consented and together they packed a knapsack with lunch, Tree got his lines and bait, and they trudged upmountain several hundred yards toward a narrow stream of cold snow-water coming from high up.

"How come everything's always *up*hill?" Vi complained, taking his hand so he could help her. "Isn't anything ever downhill?"

"Nothing worthwhile," Tree replied matter-of-factly.

Vi started to debate that with him, but changed her mind. He had said it too naturally; somehow she knew that he meant it.

They walked along the stream and Tree showed her how to set fish lines without poles or other apparatus. "Poles scare off fish," he explained. "They cast a shadow over the water."

When he had the lines set, they walked on to a point where the stream bed dropped six feet, creating a low waterfall. There the water rushed and formed whitecaps, and occasionally they could see a mountain trout swimming upstream, actually jumping up the falling water. They found a place to open the knapsack and eat. While they were there, Vi told him about herself.

"I was one of those young girls with stars in her eyes who went out to California to get into the movies. Or TV. Or modeling. *Anything,* you know, except the nine-to-five office bit. Took me a while to realize that I wasn't the only one with big ideas. There were hundreds of others just like me. We were all pilgrims who made it to Mecca—only Mecca turned out to be Hustle City. I was lucky; I ended up waiting tables at a Hamburger Hamlet. A lot of others weren't lucky: they ended up on drugs, or selling themselves on Hollywood Boulevard for some pimp, or even worse. That's why when the two sports in the Cadillac asked if I wanted a ride east, I took it."

"No modeling job at Marshall Field's?"

Vi shook her head. "Most I've got to look forward to is a monotonous job in some dull office."

"That's more than some people have got," Tree commented darkly.

Again she started to question him. And again she changed her mind.

That night, her third night at the cabin, Tree let her cook for him. She made breaded pork chops from his freezer, and managed to whip up some decent mashed potatoes from his dehydrated food stock.

"Not bad," he said. "Where'd you learn to cook?"

"Marshall High School, on the west side of Chicago. Home Ec was required. Where'd you go to school?"

"A reservation in Idaho."

"What was it like, living on a reservation?"

"Poor," he said quietly. "Cold poor. Hungry poor. Hard-knock poor."

"How'd you get away from it?"

"Joined the army." He realized the slip at once.

Wild Things

"You told me you came up here to evade the draft," she reminded him.

Tree looked down at the table for a long silent moment. Finally he met her eyes. "That was a lie. But I can't tell you the truth. Let's just leave it alone for the rest of the time you're here, okay?"

They resumed eating, with no further conversation for several minutes. Finally Vi put her fork down and rose.

"I told you the truth about me," she said. It was clearly an accusation. She left the table and went outside.

Tree finished his supper, cleared off the table, and washed the dishes. Then he got an apple out of the food locker for Elk and went outside. Vi was sitting on the porch looking up at a sky full of stars that looked close enough to touch.

"Want to feed this apple to Elk?" Tree asked.

"Elk doesn't like me," Vi said.

"She's just not used to you. Come on, you can feed her." Vi did not move. Tree coaxed her. "Come on. I'll show you how. It's easy. Come on."

Finally Vi got up and went with him around to the lean-to. Tree cut the apple into sixths and showed Vi how to hold her hand out straight, palm up, so that the horse could take the food with its lips and not hurt Vi's hand with its powerful teeth. Vi was nervous, but Elk, whose affections could always be bought with fresh apples, played the perfect lady and ate properly.

"Go ahead, scratch her neck," Tree said. "She likes that."

"Don't we all," Vi replied, mostly to herself.

Vi petted the Appaloosa for awhile, then Tree closed the stall and they returned to the porch.

"I'll let you help me feed the wild things in the morning if you like," he offered.

"You don't have to."

"I don't want you to be mad."

"I'm not. I don't blame you for not trusting me."

"It's not that I don't trust you. It's just something I don't talk about. Not to anybody."

She was sitting in a shaft of light from the window and Tree saw her shrug. "Okay," she said.

"I'm sorry."

Another shrug. "Sure."

They sat without speaking for ten minutes, listening to the night sounds of the cool, high-mountain evening. Finally Vi stood up.

"I think I'll go to bed. Goodnight."

"Goodnight."

Tree remained on the porch for a long time, thinking about things: the vivid, dangerous past; the nebulous, unsure future; and the clear, demanding present. He admitted to himself that he wanted the woman, then told himself in definite, forceful language—silently, in his head—that he could not have her. Alone is safest, he reminded himself. Alone is smartest. Alone is best.

He grunted softly. Alone was also loneliest.

It was midnight when he finally went inside, stripped down, and slid into his sleeping bag. But he could not sleep. It was as if he were waiting for something.

He was still awake when she came to him in the darkness.

On Wednesday morning he let her help him feed the wild things. At first they were skittish about her, made nervous by the sight and scent of her so close. But because they trusted Tree so completely, they gradually eased their way up to her. Soon she was kneeling in their midst just as Tree did, and they were nuzzling her hands, putting front paws up on her legs, making their individual little noises to get her attention. She learned that the mule deer and the pronghorn would nibble at her ears with their lips if she paid too much attention to the ground animals and not enough to them. Feeding the wild things was a decided thrill for Vi; she could not wait for the next day to feed them again.

"I want to feed them every morning!" she said with delight. Tree looked curiously at her and Vi's smile faded. "Oh, I forgot," she said. "I've only got two more mornings, haven't I? The bus comes over the mountain on Friday."

Tree nodded. "Yes. On Friday."

They went swimming that afternoon, in the same stream in which they had fished the previous day. Vi thought she was going to freeze.

"It's like ice water!" she shrieked.

"It *is* ice water," Tree said, laughing. "It's melted snow from 'way up. Move around; you'll get warm."

She did move around, but she did not warm up. After five minutes she had to get out. Tree wrapped her in a blanket and left her on the bank while he swam for another quarter-hour. When he came out, his tan body shone like the coats of the wild things who were his friends.

After their swim, they walked arm-in-arm back to the cabin and Tree built a fire. They stretched out on a Navajo blanket in front of the fireplace, chewed some peyote, slept, woke up and made love, and slept again.

That night, Tree said, "You don't want to leave, do you?"

Vi shrugged. "I don't want to mess with your life, Tree. You've got everything you want up here. The one thing you haven't got—well, it's available down on the Salmon River Reservation when you want it, and you don't have to bring it home with you." She looked away from him. "I think it would be bad for both of us if I stayed."

They did not discuss it any further that night, each retreating into silence.

On Thursday morning, Tree was sick.

"My cooking," Vi said lightly. "Now you know why I've never married."

"Probably the peyote," he told her. "It gives you a great feeling, but sometimes it raises hell with the digestive system. How's your stomach?"

"Fine. Let me mix you some cold powdered milk; that'll probably settle it."

The milk helped some, but later in the day he had severe nausea and a bad headache.

"Do you have any medicine up here at all?" Vi asked. He directed her to a cabinet in the kitchen where he had aspirin, codeine, and Valium tablets. She gave him two of each and made him take a nap in the bedroom.

While he was sleeping, she went to the bookcase and took down the scrapbook he had hidden on top of it. She had watched through the window the night he had put it there. Opening it on the table she read the newspaper clippings he had saved. The stories they told were different, but they all had common headlines:

LABOR LEADER SLAIN, one read.
GANGLAND BOSS FOUND DEAD, read another.
WITNESS MURDERED IN HOTEL.
RACKETS INFORMER EXECUTED.
GAMBLER KILLED IN MIAMI.

The clippings had datelines covering a five-year period—the last one was dated six years earlier.

Tree came out of the bedroom while she still had the scrapbook open in front of her. He was very pale, but his eyes were still dark and dangerous. He was fully dressed and Vi could not tell whether he had his gun or not. He sat down heavily across from her.

"You enjoy my press notices?" he asked.

Vi closed the scrapbook. "They ended six years ago. That was when you came to live up here. What happened?"

"They wanted me to hit a woman," he said. "A young woman with a brace on one leg, who was going into a convent of handicapped nuns, who taught handicapped children. She was heir to a lot of money, but she was going to take a vow of poverty and give it all to the order she was joining. A cousin who was her only living relative bought the hit. Prior to then, I had never hit anybody but gangsters and punks, a stoolie now and then, a gambler who welshed on somebody. Now they wanted me to do a crippled young woman who never hurt nobody. They wanted me to run her down in the street so it'd look like a hit-and-run, an accident." Tree shook his head. "I couldn't do it. So I took off."

"And now there's a contract on you," Vi concluded.

"A big one," Tree confirmed. "And it keeps getting bigger every year." Suddenly he buried his face in his hands. "I'm sick, Vi—" he said weakly.

She helped him back to bed, mixed him some more powdered milk, and made him eat a few soda crackers to see if that would help calm his stomach. Sitting on the bed beside him, she felt his forehead. "No fever," she reported.

"Maybe it's the flu," he said. "My muscles and joints ache like hell."

After he ate, she massaged him where he hurt and gave him more aspirin and Valium. Then she tucked him in and stroked his cheek.

"How'd you get to be a—you know," she asked curiously.

"A paid killer?" Tree smiled wanly. "In the army. I was a POW. Did time with a Ranger captain who had mob connections. When we were exchanged and sent home, he asked me to work for him. It sounded better than going back to the reservation." He reached up and touched her hand. "You won't go tomorrow, will you?"

"No. I won't leave you while you're sick."

He had a miserable night. Between bouts of diarrhea and vomiting, he was left weak and shaky. She helped him to and from bed, gave him more medication, more milk, more crackers. His muscle and joint aches agonized him all through the night; even codeine tablets failed to curb the pain. Toward morning he still had no fever, but his pulse had become very weak and his eyes no longer looked threatening. When Vi took the gun from under his pillow, where she had noticed it, he did not complain; he knew he did not have the strength to fire it anyway. Still, he was relieved to see her merely lay it on the nearby bureau and leave it there.

Two hours after sun-up, he was breathing very lightly and was extremely pale. She was holding his head up, feeding him a little warm oatmeal.

"Feed—the—wild things—" he said feebly.

"I will," she assured him. "After I feed you. You're sick, they're not. Come on, open—"

When he had eaten as much as she thought he could, she let his head back down and wiped his face with a damp cloth. She opened a window for him to get some fresh air, and cleaned up the dishes they had used during the night. When she came back in to check on him, he was barely awake. Just enough to say faintly, "The—wild—things—"

"All right," she said. "I'll do it right now."

He gave her a faint smile. She bent and kissed him lightly on the lips.

Out back, Vi got a bucket of pellet food from the storage locker and went over to where the wild things waited. She held out her hand to them, but they would not come. They merely stared at her. She tossed a handful of food to them, but they did not touch it. Maybe they smell the arsenic on my hands, she thought.

Vi shrugged, poured the bucket of food on the ground, and went back inside to see if Tree was in a coma yet.

The scene here is New Orleans, and one of the main characters is a troubled Dixieland jazz musician, much like the one in **HORN MAN,** *the first New Orleans story I wrote, which was honored with the Edgar Allan Poe Award in 1981. Dixieland jazz, like boxing, is another thing in life that I learned to love when I was young, in Memphis, near the little town where I was born.*

The musician in this story, Lew McCulla, has, like boxer Dave Handley in **HIT AND RUN,** *a hard choice to make: do what he does best, the only thing he knows how to do, in the face of dangerous odds against him, and possible dire consequences if he is successful.*

Plus, he has one other worry: his kid, a street-wise young boy whose name we never learn . . .

McCulla's Kid

Old Rainey found McCulla's kid in a drugstore on Royal Street, buying brown polish to restock his shoeshine box.

"Whar' yo' daddy at?" Rainey asked him.

"Sleeping," McCulla's kid said.

"I done knocked on the door," Rainey said. "Didn't get no answer."

The kid glanced away. "Sometimes he sleeps pretty sound."

I'll bet he do, Rainey thought. 'Specially when he's drunk. Rainey bent his old black face next to the white boy's ear. He didn't have to bend far—he'd been walking with a stoop since he was seventy. "I wants you to come unlock the door for me," he told the boy, "so's I can wake him up. Mr. Gaston wants to talk to him over at the Hall right away."

McCulla's Kid

The "Hall" was Tradition Hall, the most famous jazz club in the *Vieux Carre*, the French Quarter of New Orleans. Mr. Gaston was its owner. McCulla's kid knew that if Mr. Gaston was sending for his dad, it must be important.

"Sure, I'll let you in," the boy told old Rainey. He paid for his tin of polish, slung his shine box over one shoulder, and he and Rainey left. They walked up Royal to Pirate's Alley, then cut past the cathedral to Jackson Square. Though early, the morning already promised a mugginess that would drive everyone, even the tourists, indoors by three o'clock. As they walked, they had little to say, this old black man and the young white boy, who was twelve. They didn't know each other well, the boy and his father having returned to the Quarter from Kansas City less than a month earlier after a long absence.

Rainey and the boy made an odd pair as they moved along: the old man bent and white-haired with age, shuffling as he walked, pursing his lips and occasionally muttering some complaint against the world in general; the boy tanned, his hair bleached yellow by the sun, blue eyes bright but not young, mouth set. They walked through Jackson Square, where several artists were already setting up their easels, and turned down Decatur.

"What you get for a shoeshine, boy?" old Rainey asked.

"Half a dollar," the kid answered.

"Half a dollar!" Rainey said indignantly. "Why, when *I* was a boy shining on this here very street, we didn't get but a *nickel*. And that was for mostly *boots* too. A nickel. That was all."

McCulla's kid shrugged his shoulders. "Half a dollar," he repeated. He wouldn't *spit* for a nickel.

In the middle of the first block on Decatur, the kid and Rainey turned into a narrow passageway between the two front buildings and went through to a rear building separated by a garden—or what had once been a garden. When the rear building had been the three-story townhouse of a wealthy upriver plantation family, the plot between the two buildings had been outrageous with crape myrtles, magnolias, camellias, redbuds, and a dozen other species of cultivated flowers that flourished in the moist semitropical air. In the cool of the evening, it had been a place to sit and take in fragrances and count blessings. But since the townhouse had become a collection of sleeping rooms and kitchenettes, and its tenants the kind to whom the garden was just something through which to pass to get to the street, it had, like the townhouse, fallen on hard times and been reduced to a state of dismal neglect. Where once had bloomed vibrantly hued flowers, there was now displayed only empty beer cans, cigarette butts, and an occasional item even more gross.

The kid and old Rainey went up a flight of outside stairs and along a balcony to a door with 2-C painted on it by an amateur hand. The kid unlocked the door and Rainey followed him inside. It was a bare, seedy little place with no signs of pride. The wooden table and three straight chairs were scratched beyond refinishing, the two-burner hotplate dangerously greasy, chintz curtains heavy with dust, floor linoleum patchy with age. On one of two folding cots in a tiny sleeping alcove, the kid's father, Lew McCulla, slept an open-mouthed, alcoholic sleep. On the floor next to his cot were an open bottle of Old Crow and a closed clarinet case.

Old Rainey started for the sleeping man, but the kid cut him off. "I'll do it," he said, and Rainey could tell by his eyes that it was not open for discussion. Unslinging the shine box, the kid dropped to his knees next to the cot and began shaking his sleeping father. "Lew," he said. "Come on, Lew, wake up—"

McCulla's Kid

Lew McCulla came out of it slowly and reluctantly, struggling for focus, fighting the taste in his mouth, testing his limbs one at a time for response. When the groping man got up as far as one elbow, the kid took the bottle and went over to the hotplate. Lighting the burner, he set a dented coffeepot over the spurts of blue flame and washed out a cup. Rainey watched all this with great, frowning interest, still fascinated after three-quarters of a century by some of the white man's mores.

"Give me a drink, kid," Lew McCulla said raspily from the cot.

"Only with some coffee," the kid said.

"Goddamnit, bring me that bottle!"

"With some coffee," the kid repeated firmly. Glancing over at his father, he decided how strong the coffee had to be. Some days were light—just hot, black coffee. Some were medium, with a spoonful of chicory. Some were heavy, after a real binge: two spoonfuls of chicory. Today Lew McCulla looked like medium would put him on his feet. The kid got down the jar of ground chicory and measured one spoonful.

"What's he doing here?" McCulla asked the kid when he realized Rainey was in the room.

"Come to get you. Mr. Gaston sent him."

McCulla squinted quizzically at Rainey. "I do something wrong last night? He fixing to fire me?"

Rainey shrugged. "Ah don't know nothin' 'cept he want you over dere."

McCulla began muttering an obscenity-laced soliloquy on the inequities of poor memory and early rising. The kid mixed a shot of whiskey in a cup of coffee and took it to him. "Hot," he warned.

"I'm not blind or stupid," McCulla said. "I can see the steam." He tried to take a sip and burned his lips. "Son of a bitch!"

"Ain't blind and ain't stupid," old Rainey muttered. "Wonder what the problem be, den."

The kid ignored the old black man's comment. He had learned long ago, when he was eight or nine, that if he defended against every slur cast at his father, he'd spend a good part of his life fighting. Sitting on the floor, he opened his shoeshine box and uncapped the new tin of brown polish to mix a little water with it for easier spreading. It would, he knew, take Lew twenty minutes to start independent functioning. Then the kid could get back out on the streets of the *Vieux Carre* and start making some money.

Mr. Gaston's office, upstairs over Tradition Hall, made no concession at all to current times. The desk lamp had a shield of antique green glass, there was a spindle instead of an OUT box, there were a fountain pen and inkwell, and on the wall there was a 1935 calendar, which matched identically the 1985 calendar, but which Gaston liked better because it featured a photograph of Dolores Del Rio.

The dapper club owner, who in his time had been everything from a bootlegger to a bookmaker, placed the tips of his manicured fingers together and studied Lew McCulla, with unblinking eyes. McCulla was one of the best pure Dixieland clarinetists Gaston had ever heard—and Gaston had heard them all. He had heard Louis Cottrell, Jr. play the "Bogalusa Strut" with the Young Tuxedoes back in the 1930s, heard Jimmy Hartwell play with Bix's Wolverines, when they did "Jazz Me Blues" in Richmond, Indiana, in 1924, and heard the legendary Jimmy Noone, the greatest communicative clarinetist in history, at the Apex Club in Chicago where Earl Hines was a young piano player. Hell, he had even heard Sidney Celestine once for a few minutes. Lew McCulla was as good as any of them—or would have been if he ever stayed sober two days running. McCulla, as far as Gaston knew, was the last of the Albert System clarinetists, still using the old-time, differently constructed and fingered instrument that so faithfully captured the pure New Orleans sound. *Why*, Gaston wondered, did the Great Dixieland Bandleader in the Sky send him such an outstanding talent, and then attach so many strings to him? It was bad enough that McCulla had a kid that the truant officers were always after because he refused to go to school, and bad enough that the only time McCulla didn't have a bottle to his lips was when the clarinet mouthpiece was there, but now Gaston found himself faced with still another problem.

"Two guys," he told McCulla in the same neutral tone he used for every occasion from ardor to death threats, "big, ugly guys. Down from Kansas City. They say you owe Calder Lingle some money. And that you skipped out. Calder sent them down here to cripple you."

McCulla sighed a deep, weary sigh and leaned forward, elbows on knees. Gaston could see perspiration emerge on the surface of his forehead.

"How much do you owe him?"

"Eight."

"I'll let you have it and take it back a hundred a week for two months, no interest."

McCulla was already shaking his head. "Not eight hundred. Eight *grand*."

Gaston and old Rainey, who was waiting by the door, exchanged incredulous looks. Eight *thousand?* "I don't believe it," Gaston said.

"Believe it," McCulla urged.

"How in the hell—"

"Don't ask. The horses. Cards. A woman named Lila Mae. The booze." He glanced from Gaston to Rainey and back, helpless and embarrassed. "Life just got away from me. I couldn't get a handle on anything."

Now it was Gaston's turn to sigh wearily. "Well, I can't stake you to eight grand—money's too tight right now. But I can let you have enough for you and the kid to split. If you want to head down Galveston way, I have a friend who owns a small jazz club there."

But again Lew McCulla was shaking his head. "I can't leave New Orleans right now. The woodwinds committee from the Jazz Hall of Fame will be in town tonight to listen to me play. I'm one of the three finalists this year. I've got a chance to be voted into the Hall of Fame."

"I don't think you quite understand," Gaston said slowly. "There's a committee of two down here from Kansas City that wants to vote you into an intensive-care unit. You've got to leave New Orleans."

"I can't." McCulla wet his lips. "You remember my wife, Mr. Gaston? Her name was Edie."

Gaston nodded. Edie had been the daughter of a tenor-sax player with the Fudge Ripples, one of the first integrated Dixieland bands. Like McCulla himself, she had grown up in the *Vieux Carre*—the sounds of Dixieland had been her bedtime lullaby. At sixteen she got pregnant by Lew McCulla, who was then twenty, and her father threatened to kill them. They ran off to one of those Southern states where the age of consent is twelve, got married, and gravitated up the muddy Mississippi to Memphis, where Lew found clarinet work on Beale Street. Their baby came—a boy—and Edie began a campaign of sending her daddy pictures of him every month. After two years, the old man forgave them and they moved back to New Orleans. For the next four years they lived an idyllic life. Then Edie started having headaches. She thought it was eye strain and got reading glasses. The headaches continued. She took aspirin. Then aspirin and codeine. Then Demerol. Finally she checked into a hospital. By that time the brain tumor causing the headaches was inoperable.

After Edie's death, Lew McCulla left New Orleans and wandered around the South, playing here, playing there, never staying in one place very long, beginning to drink a lot. He played in beer bars and roadhouses and dance clubs in places with names like Hattiesburg, Tuscaloosa, and Waycross, always dragging the kid along with him, letting him grow up in diners, pool halls, bus depots. Sometimes the kid got in a full month of school somewhere before they moved on, sometimes not. He learned to read a little, spell a little, make change, and lie a lot. Along the line his eyes turned hard and he became a survivor. He watched his father play clarinet so often that he knew every finger movement of every Dixieland standard that Lew McCulla played, yet he would never touch the instrument. He told his father he didn't like music. It was actually the musician's life, the way his father lived it, that he didn't like.

Most people who were associated with Dixieland in the *Vieux Carre* knew the story of Lew McCulla and his kid, and remembered Edie McCulla. A roundy, smiling, effervescent girl, she had liked everyone and everyone had liked her. Gaston remembered her well.

"What's she got to do with you not being able to leave New Orleans?" he asked McCulla.

Lew wet his lips. "I'm not sure you'll understand this, but see, Edie was very proud of my playing. She thought the music I made with my clarinet was the most beautiful sound in the world. She wanted the kid to be a musician someday, too. I used to tell her what if he don't want to? What if he wants to be something else? But she always said, 'Just make him proud of you, Lew. Do that and he'll want to be just like you.' "

Gaston began to understand. "You think making the Jazz Hall of Fame will do it?"

McCulla shrugged. "It's worth a try. Nothing else has ever worked." He looked down at the floor. "I'm not much of an example any other way."

Gaston was silent for a moment. Then he asked, "When were you nominated?"

"Three months ago. Even with all the problems up in K. C., I still managed to work steady. I played with Rick Ellsworth's band at the Blue River club. That's where the woodwinds nominating committee caught me. They had a list of twelve guys who'd been in the business for at least ten years, which is a requirement. During the last few months, they've narrowed the list down to three."

"Who are you up against?"

"Grover Washington, Jr., and Zoot Sims."

"That's heavy competition."

A hint of a smile came to Lew McCulla's lip. It was a smile that said he knew how good he was. "If you don't think I've got a chance," he told Gaston, "I'll go ahead and split."

"Don't get cute with me, McCulla," the older man said. "You know you're good enough to win, and you know I know it. Question is, can you stay out of the hospital long enough to win?"

"I got to try, Mr. Gaston," Lew said, all pretense gone now. "For Edie, I got to try."

Gaston and old Rainey exchanged looks again. They had known each other for thirty years and their minds usually reached the same conclusions, though frequently for different reasons. Right now they were thinking: *trouble*. Gaston was blaming one thing: *musicians*. Old Rainey another: *white folks*. But both knew they would help Lew McCulla however they could. He was part of the Quarter, and so were they.

That meant something.

"Maybe," Gaston said, "we can let the Hall of Fame committee hear you and still get you out of town. Where's the committee staying?"

"The Royal Orleans. They're coming to Tradition Hall at eight for the first set."

"The two guys from Kansas City will be here for the first set, too. We've got to fix it so you won't be here." Gaston reached for an old-fashioned black telephone, lifted the receiver, and jiggled the hook. "Get me Virgil's on Basin Street," he told his switchboard operator. A moment later he said, "Virgil, this is Gaston. You've got Peanuts Kenner playing clarinet with your bunch over there, right? Okay, here's what I want you to do. Send Peanuts over here to play tonight and let my clarinetist Lew McCulla sit in with your guys. We're trying to keep McCulla away from some outsiders who're after him."

The word "outsiders" always worked magic in the Quarter: Virgil agreed at once. When Gaston hung up, he said to old Rainey, "Get over to the Royal Orleans and tell the Hall of Fame committee McCulla will be at Virgil's on Basin Street instead of here."

As soon as Rainey left, Gaston took two hundred dollars out of his pocket and handed it to McCulla. "Soon's those committee people hear you, take the kid and split for Galveston. My friend's place is the Lone Star Club, on the Strand. I'll call him."

"Thanks, Mr. Gaston," McCulla said, sheepish and ashamed, "I owe you."

Watching McCulla leave, Gaston thought, sure, sure—you and a hundred other ragtimers. One thing Gaston had learned over the years was that Dixieland musicians never paid their debts. As a group, they were probably the most irresponsible people who ever walked upright. Absolutely worthless. Their only redeeming value, as far as Gaston was concerned, was that they played the sweetest music this side of heaven.

The two apes from Kansas City came back to Gaston's office at five past eight, just after Tradition Hall's first set had begun. One ape watched, while one talked.

"Like I tol' you earlier, Mr. Gaston, we represent Mr. Calder Lingle of Kansas City. Mr. Lingle sent us after this licorice stick player named McCulla that welshed on a bundle of dough. We come down here to learn him a lesson. He's supposed to be playing at your joint, but he ain't here. We need to find him. Mr. Lingle tol' us you'd cooperate."

"I'll see what I can do," Gaston said. He picked up a small brass servant's bell and shook it several times. The two apes exchanged dubious glances. Presently a woman of about forty with a Rubenesque figure, wearing a 1920s shimmy dress, came in. Gaston asked about McCulla.

"He's sick," the woman replied, as rehearsed. "From the booze most likely. We got a replacement from the union hall."

"Get me his address," Gaston instructed. The woman left and returned a moment later with McCulla's address on Decatur. It was the actual address—with Calder Lingle involved, Gaston had to make his cooperation look legitimate. "You can probably catch him at home," he said handing over the address. "Let me know if there's anything else I can do." The head ape thanked him. As they were leaving, Gaston said to the woman, loudly enough for them to hear, "Tell the union hall we'll need a permanent replacement clarinetist as soon as possible."

At Virgil's on Basin Street, the first set of the evening

began with "Dipper-mouth Blues," and without pause went into "Panama" and "Sweet Lorraine." The Hall of Fame committee had not arrived. Virgil, the club owner, and old Rainey, who had been sent by Gaston to fill him in on the story, stood off to the side of the bandstand watching the front door.

"You sure they got the message that McCulla would be playing here instead of over at Tradition?" Virgil asked. Old Rainey nodded emphatically.

"I deliver dat message myself. Dey be along." He turned and started to shuffle away.

"Where are you going?"

"Over to where he live," Rainey said bobbing his chin at McCulla. "Mr. Gaston, he be sending dem thugs over dere. He want me to make sure de boy ain't around."

"Boy? Oh, McCulla's kid."

"Dat's right," Rainey replied. He shuffled around behind the bandstand and out the back door.

McCulla's kid was at the scarred old table in the little apartment on Decatur, eating pork and beans from an open can and saltine crackers from a box, drinking Dr. Pepper, and counting his money. He had, all in change, four dollars and twenty cents, representing seven shines that afternoon, plus tips. As he ate, he neatly stacked the money on the table—nickels, dimes, quarters and halves. In a little dime-store spiral notebook he used a pencil stub to enter $3.20 after a column of figures that covered half the pages in the book. Carefully adding that entry to the last figure, he wrote a new total: $612.60. Then he put the book and all but one dollar in change into a LeMoyne Coffee can on a shelf under the hotplate. The can already contained nearly ten dollars that he had put in it since the week began. Every Friday he took the money to the Louisiana Bank on Canal Street and deposited it in a savings account. He had been saving for almost a year. In another nine months, he hoped to have one thousand dollars saved. Then he was going to put Lew in the Chelsea Hills Sanitarium and have him cured of the booze.

With the coffee can back on the shelf, the kid returned to the table and finished his solitary supper. From an open window of the apartment he could hear Dixieland music begin playing as the first set started at the Ursuline Club around the corner. The opening number was "Sweet Sue." The kid had watched Lew play that number a hundred times over the years. Closing his eyes, he pictured a clarinet with fingers moving exactly as they should to produce each note perfectly.

As the kid ate, the unseen band moved into "Davenport Blues," which Hoagy Carmichael had written in tribute to Bix Beiderbecke, and then into "Lonesome Road," which opened with a long, lugubrious clarinet solo. Lonesome Road, the kid knew, had been his mother's favorite song. The kid's grandfather, before he died, had told him that. He had told the kid many stories about Edie, mostly of her as a little girl growing up in the *Vieux Carre*. The old man's stories had made the Quarter sound like some wonderland filled with happy music being played by and for special people. The kid knew differently. The Quarter was a dark, shadowy place where you had to scratch for every dime you made, and where there was always someone lurking about looking to take it from you. When the kid had his thousand dollars saved, and got Lew cured of the booze, he hoped they could leave New Orleans and never return.

Finishing his supper, the kid tossed his pork-and-beans and Dr. Pepper cans into a sack under the sink, rinsed off his spoon, and carefully closed the waxed paper to keep the

McCulla's Kid

crackers from going stale. Slinging his shine box, he left the apartment and went downstairs, trying to decide where to work that night. Most of the nighttime tourists head for Bourbon, which was closed to vehicular traffic at night and became a kind of tourist mall, but the tough black kids had decided that Bourbon was theirs—white shoeshine boys caught there had their shine boxes smashed and their money taken. The kid decided to try Bienville Street, where the whores hung out. Lots of times a john would let you give him a shine while he was looking over the parade of flesh.

As the kid was passing through the garden, he saw a figure in the grayness of the areaway leading to the street. Instinctively, he reached into his back pocket where he carried a switchblade.

"It's me, boy," old Rainey said. "Lea' that blade be."

"What do you want?" McCulla's kid asked.

"I brang a message from yo' daddy. He say tell you he ain't at Tradition tonight—he settin' in at Virgil's on Basin Street instead."

"Okay," the kid said. It wasn't unusual—Dixieland musicians often traded chairs for an evening. It was a break from the routine of playing in the same house night after night.

"Whar' you going to now?" Rainey asked.

"Iberville Street," the kid lied. He didn't like anyone knowing where he was.

"I'se going to Toulouse," Rainey said. "I walk wid you dat far."

"Suit yourself," the kid said.

They went off down the street together.

The two apes from Kansas City passed the old black man and the boy on their way to the address Gaston had given them. They went through the garden, found the right apartment, and shouldered the door open without even knocking. The building manager heard the noise and came to investigate.

"We're looking for Lew McCulla," the ape that talked said. "We're cops."

"Jeez, did you have to break the lock?" the manager complained. "Are you sure you're cops?"

"Positive." The ape reached into his pocket and the manager thought he was going to produce a badge. Instead, he handed the manager a fifty.

"Have the lock fixed and keep the change. Can you tell us where McCulla is? He called in sick at work."

"Jeez, I don't know," the manager said with a frown. "He left at his usual time, carrying his clarinet case like always. You sure he ain't at Tradition Hall?"

"Positive. Any idea where he might have gone?"

"Jeez, no. His kid might know, but you just missed him. He left a couple of minutes ago with his shoeshine box. You might catch him on the street."

The apes exchanged looks, remembering the kid and the old man they had just passed. They hurried back out and started looking up and down Decatur Street.

At Virgil's on Basin Street, the Jazz Hall of Fame woodwinds committee arrived at twenty of nine.

"Center table in the back, just like you requested on the phone, gentlemen," Virgil said, escorting them across the club. "I was beginning to think you weren't coming."

"We always arrive late," one of the trio said. "It gives the musician we've come to see time to warm up. We don't feel it's fair to listen to a cold instrument."

"That's what I call very considerate," Virgil said, impressed. He himself was a musician. It was obvious to him that these men understood what playing was all about. Virgil snapped his fingers for a waiter. "Bring these gentlemen anything they want," he instructed, "and give the check to me."

Virgil retreated to his office and telephoned Gaston. "They're finally here," he told the Tradition Hall owner.

In his office, Gaston snapped open an old-fashioned pocket watch. Looking at the time, he knew Virgil's band would be on their first break of the evening. "What's their lead-in on the second set?" he inquired.

Virgil thought for a second, then replied, " 'Snake Rag,' 'High Society,' and 'Savoy Blues.' "

"Have them substitute 'Muskrat Ramble' for 'Snake Rag,' " he suggested. "It's a more familiar piece and the gentlemen on the committee will be able to identify it more easily. It has a better clarinet part for McCulla, too."

Virgil agreed. After hanging up, he went into the alley where the band took its break and made the change in the program. None of the musicians questioned it—they assumed it was a request from one of the customers. Before Virgil could go back inside, Lew McCulla came over to him.

"They here yet?"

"They're here."

Virgil went back into the club. McCulla leaned up against the brick of the building and started to take a drink from a pint bottle in a paper bag. Then he thought of the committee. And of Edie. He wanted the drink very badly. But there was something he wanted more: his name in the Jazz Hall of Fame. For the kid.

Closing the bottle, he put it back in his coat pocket.

The apes from Kansas city searched up and down Decatur, Ursuline, St. Philip, and Chartres streets, but couldn't find McCulla's kid or the old black man with whom they'd seen him. The one that talked cursed, and they went looking for a pay phone to call Kansas City. They found one near the Cafe du Monde across from Jackson Square.

"Mr. Lingle," the one ape said when the call got through, "that licorice-stick player ain't working tonight and ain't in his apartment. So far we ain't leaned on nobody to find him 'cause you said no strong-arm except on McCulla hisself. You want we should hang around or what?"

"Hang on a minute," Calder Lingle said in a raspy voice at the other end. The ape heard him say to someone in his office, "Get Kid Benoit in here." Kid Benoit, the ape knew, was the leader of the jazz band at the club where Lingle had his office. Several moments later, the ape heard Lingle say, "Kid, what was it you were telling us earlier about some jazz committee being in New Orleans to hear McCulla play?" The ape heard Benoit's voice in the background but couldn't make out what he was saying. Presently Lingle said, "Okay, thanks, Kid," and came back on the line. "Check the Quarter hotels," he instructed. "Look for three guys representing the Jazz Hall of Fame. Find them, you'll find McCulla. Don't waste no time." He hung up.

At the pay phone, the ape opened the classified directory and ripped out the page listing the *Vieux Carre* hotels. They were all within a few blocks radius, so it wouldn't take long to check them.

The woodwinds committee remained at Virgil's for an hour and a half, listening to two complete sets. They heard McCulla play a full range of Dixieland numbers, from the basic clarinet exercise in "Eccentric" and the soft, soulful passages in "Never Touched Me," to a lively intertwining with Frog Norman's slide trombone in "Tin Roof Blues," and a masterful, unbelievably long concluding note in "Tiger

McCulla's Kid

Rag." It was a bravura performance that drew wild applause from the audience and rounds of compliments from the other musicians during the band's second and third breaks. McCulla surprised even himself. He hadn't played that sober in years, or that well. God, if only Edie had heard him tonight! Then again, he thought, glancing up at the black sky from the alley during their break, maybe she had.

As a courtesy to the woodwinds committee, Mr. Gaston picked them up in his chauffeured limousine when they were ready to leave Virgil's. The limousine was a 1937 Packard V-12 with bulletproof windows, as brand-new in appearance as it had been when it belonged to Ralph "Bottles" Capone, Big Al's brother, back in Chicago, before Gaston had acquired it from a subsequent owner.

"This is very kind of you, Mr. Gaston," the committee chairman said as they rode back to the Royal Orleans. "It seems an appropriate moment for us to express our gratitude for your continued financial support of the Jazz Hall of Fame. Needless to say, without generosity such as yours, the Hall wouldn't exist."

"My pleasure, gentlemen," Gaston said. "I suppose it would be unethical for me to ask how your voting will go this year?"

"I'm afraid it would, yes," the chairman replied. He exchanged smiles with the other two members of the committee. "We can certainly discuss music in general, however, as friends. My associates and I were just agreeing as we left the club that none of us had ever heard a better clarinet performance than we heard tonight. Never. And," he emphasized, "we've already listened to the other two nominees."

Gaston sat back and added his own pleased smile to theirs.

An hour later, after Tradition Hall closed for the night,

Peanuts Kenner, the regular clarinetist from Virgil's, found the band in the alley on a break after their fourth set. He went over to McCulla, who was finally allowing himself to take a drink.

"How'd it go tonight, my man?" Peanuts asked.

"Real good," McCulla replied. "Everything okay over at Tradition?"

"Pure notes all the way. You heading out now?"

"Yeah, soon's I collect my kid. Heading for—"

"Don't tell me, bro," Peanuts interrupted. He put out his hand. "Just play it mellow, wherever."

McCulla shook hands with him. "Thanks, man."

When the band went back for the fifth set, Peanuts took his regular chair while McCulla cased his clarinet, thanked and said goodbye to Virgil, and left by the kitchen door. Walking down the narrow alley, McCulla couldn't help smiling, thinking how well he had played. He had hit notes tonight, and *held* them, and reached a clarity and quality and achieved a vibrato like he had heard Sidney Bechet do when Bechet played with Noble Sissle and McCulla had been about the age his own kid was now. What a feeling that had been! God, he thought, looking up at the sky again, Edie just *had* to have been listening.

It was as McCulla was looking up at the sky that the first ape hit him, real low and real hard, and McCulla doubled up and slipped to his knees, dropping his clarinet case. One ape pulled him to his feet from behind and held his arms while the other methodically worked him over with both hands like he was a heavy bag in a gym. Most of the blows were to the diamond formed by McCulla's waist and two hipbones. There were occasional diversions to his lips and nose and cheeks, to draw some external blood, but the ape doing the punching was too professional to damage his knuckles and stayed mainly in the soft areas, counting on the ruptures and internal bleeding he knew he was causing. He worked on McCulla for five minutes, until he figured the musician had taken eight thousand dollars worth, then he and his partner left the unconscious man face down, arms stretched over his head, in the dark shadows of the alley.

It was half an hour later that a man on his way to work a night shift backed his car out of the garage and without even knowing it, ran one rear tire over both of McCulla's hands.

Old Rainey found McCulla's kid just before midnight at the corner of Bienville and Royal.

"You tol' me you gon' be working on Iberville," he accused.

"Changed my mind," the kid said. "What do you want now?"

Rainey pursed his lips and chewed silently on some words before finally saying, "Mr. Gaston, he tol' me to see you got home tonight."

The kid's eyes instantly flashed suspicion. "What's happened?" he asked.

"Yo' daddy got beat up. He in the Orleans Parish Hospital." The kid started to hurry away but Rainey grabbed his arm. "Hold on, now! You can't get in to see him. He in what dey calls 'tensive care. Dey ain't let nobody in 'cept Mr. Gaston."

The kid sat down on an outside windowsill and stared at the sidewalk. Rainey sat beside him, chewing on words again.

"Mr. Gaston, he say for you to go on home and go to bed. He say I brang you to see him in de morning and he take you to the hospital wif him."

The kid kept staring at the sidewalk, saying nothing. He looked much older than his twelve years.

Finally Rainey asked, "You gon' do what Mr. Gaston say?"

"Yeah, okay," the kid said, rising and slinging his shine box. "Come on."

Rainey walked with him back to the apartment on Decatur. Neither of them noticed the broken lock. Rainey waited while the kid washed and got ready for bed. "You gon' be all right by yo'self?"

"Sure. I been alone before."

Rainey nodded. "I come by and get you in de morning."

The old black man left. As soon as he did, the kid got back up and dressed.

When he got to the hospital, the kid looked on the floor directory and saw that Intensive Care was on two. He sneaked up the fire stairs. It was now past one A.M. and the corridors were empty and quiet. All the nurses were at a lighted island in the middle of the long hall. The kid checked seven rooms before finally finding his father.

McCulla was lying on his back with tubes in both arms and both nostrils, and some kind of a hose in a hole in his side. The latter was attached to a nearby machine which made a soft, purring noise. He had huge, balloon-like bandages at the end of each arm.

After the kid had been standing by the bed for a minute, McCulla opened his eyes and smiled faintly. "Hiya, kid. I been waiting for you. I knew you'd get in. What kept you?"

The kid swallowed dryly. "I was working."

"Have a good night?"

"Okay. 'Bout four bucks." He looked over at the machine. "What's that for?"

"My kidneys are messed up," McCulla said. He paused a beat, then added, "Messed up bad." He saw that the kid was

McCulla's Kid

fighting tears, and wished there was an easier way to do what he had to do. But there wasn't. "That ain't the worst of it, either," he said. He bobbed his chin at the two bandages. "They had to take off my hands."

The kid lowered his chin and closed his eyes. He refused to let himself cry. Constricting his throat and neck, he stood rigid as a statue.

"Gaston was in earlier," McCulla said. "Guess what he told me? I'm gonna be in the Jazz Hall of Fame. How do you like that, kid, your old man in the Jazz Hall of Fame?"

"Far out," the kid managed to say.

They fell silent, man and boy, for several long minutes, each with his own grief, his own agony. Then McCulla said, "I been thinking. A clarinet player without hands can't count on much work, know what I mean? So before you leave, I want you to unplug that machine over there. Will you do that for me?"

The kid shook his head. "No." He looked up and saw tears trickling down his father's cheeks.

"Please, kid," McCulla begged. "It ain't just because of the hands, the music I'll never play again. It's because I've been so lonely, for so long. I want to be with your mother again. Help me, kid. Please."

The kid went over and unplugged the machine. When he got back to the bed, McCulla nodded toward his clarinet case, on a chair by the door.

"That's yours if you want it."

"I don't," the kid said.

His father nodded. "Sure, I understand. I don't blame you. Listen, you better beat it now. I'm getting kind of drowsy."

The kid nodded and walked toward the door.

"So long, kid. Take care of yourself."

"Sure."

He left without taking the clarinet case.

A few minutes later, after McCulla had died, his kid sneaked back in and got the case.

Hardhead.

It's a term used in military camps, jails, poolrooms, boxing gyms, and other sundry places where men gather who are cold-eyed, short-fused, grimly determined about something, and pretty much disinclined to entertain any notion that whatever it is they've got their mind made up about could even remotely be wrong.

There have been some legendary hardheads in American fiction, like John Steinbeck's "Tom Joad" and James Jones's "Robert E. Lee Prewitt" and W. R. Burnett's "Dix Handley." Invariably they are hillbillies, rednecks, Okies, or cowboys, and usually they are in conflict with a boss, a guard, a government, or a mean woman. They are their own worst enemy, and never seem to win, except in their own minds—which is all that matters to them.

Being a hardhead in life is not easy. I know. So does the good old boy in this story. . . .

Hanging It on a Limb

Maynard was surprised that the old Plymouth ran as well as it did. He had bought it at a junk car lot that morning for ninety dollars, just an hour after he was let out of Jackson Prison; now, after driving it nearly two hundred miles south down the length of Georgia, it was still cruising along without even an engine knock. Maybe, Maynard thought, after the six years I done, I've got some luck coming.

He decided not to count on it, however. Especially since he might have to shoot a man before the day was out.

When he crossed the line into Bunker County, Maynard let up on the accelerator a little. With the window rolled down, one prison-white arm resting on the door, he breathed in the moist, heavy air that smelled of dry earth. It should have been the heavy, musky smell of green cotton bolls warming in the afternoon sun, incubating their soft, fluffy embryos, their money crop, but for the third summer out of five Georgia had been shrouded in a drought so bad that farmers couldn't even grow string beans in their gardens, much less cotton in their fields. On both sides of the narrow state highway, Maynard saw land that was burned and stunted. Old Mother Nature, he thought. A wallowing whore one year, giving everything, and a lock-kneed little virgin the next, not even letting a poor farmer cop a feel.

Just over the county line, Maynard turned into a secondary road, a blacktop with waves of heat rising from it, and a weathered sign that read: ELMO 3. He drove half that distance, then pulled off on the shoulder in front of a timeworn frame house with a rusted tin roof and front porch that was sinking at one end. An old black man sat in a wooden rocking chair with a guitar on his lap, quietly strumming without looking down. When Maynard got out and slammed the car door, the old man's fingers stopped. His head did not turn toward the car. Maynard started along a gravel path leading from the road to the porch. The old man frowned at the sound of Maynard's footsteps.

When Maynard reached the porch, the old man, whose eyes were covered with cataracts as big as bee stings, said, "Jus' give me a minute, now. I'll get it."

As Maynard stood waiting, the front door opened and a black woman of sixty or so, two decades younger than the old man, came out. A lighter-skinned boy of about ten was with her. Neither of them spoke.

Finally the old man said confidently, "You Mason Dixon Maynard's grandson."

Hanging It on a Limb

"You got me," Maynard acknowledged, shaking his head in wonder. "I swear, I don't know how you do it, Luther. You ain't heard me walk up that path in six years."

"You mos' fooled me," Luther admitted. "Yo' step's heavier. You get fat?"

"Prison shoes," Maynard explained. Luther smiled widely.

"Did you hang it on a limb, boy?" he asked hopefully.

"No, I done my time," Maynard said.

"Yo' granddaddy and me, we hung it on a limb once," Luther said.

"Daddy," the woman interjected, "Mayne's heard that story ten dozen times since he was a boy."

"It was back in Nineteen-and-Twenty-nine," Luther continued unabashed. "Yo' granddaddy and me, we was serving on the Duvall County chain gang. He was doing two years for robbin' the cotton gin, and I was doing five for batt'ry on a white man. We was bof' from Bunker County, so we decides to hang our shackles on a limb and come home. Yo' grandmamma, she brung a piece of hacksaw blade one Sunday visitin' day and we commence taking turns carrying it back to the barracks of a night. In them days, whites and blacks was separated, even on the chain gang. Every night, one of us would saw a little bit off'n his link, then fill it with mud and let it dry. Took us almos' a month, but one day we finally ready. I ax yo' granddaddy why he want to take a black man with him. He said, 'Luther, I ain't studying yo' color. We be bof' from Bunker County, and we's going home together.' That very day, we sneak around back of the rock quarry outhouse, saw on through bof' links, then we hung our shackles on a limb and cut out. Two nights later we was eating black-eyed peas and salt pork right here in this very house." Luther smiled widely. "Them days, they never come after you, see? Long as you didn't get in no mo' trouble, you stayed free. Me and yo' granddaddy, we walk the straight and narrow from that day forth."

"You mean you never got caught at nothing after that," Maynard amended wryly.

"Sit down, Mayne," the woman said before Luther could go on. "I'll get you some nice cold tea."

"Thank you, Ella."

As she went inside, Maynard sat in one of the straight chairs near the rocker, and Luther began to strum the guitar again and softly hum a blues song. The boy, who had a *cafe au lait* complexion, studied Maynard for a moment, then asked, "Are you my daddy?"

Frowning, Maynard replied, "No, boy, I ain't nobody's daddy."

The boy went out into the yard and sat on an old stump, drawing one knee up and swinging the other foot restlessly. While they were alone, Maynard pulled a pint bottle of White Lightning from his hip pocket and quickly took a long swallow. Capping the bottle, he put it Luther's hand. "Little present," he whispered.

"Fac'try liquor?" the blind man asked, his fingers feeling the label.

"Yeah. 'Bout half full."

Luther quickly slipped the bottle inside his shirt and resumed strumming. Presently, Ella returned with Maynard's iced tea.

"How's it been with y'all, Ella?" Maynard asked, taking a drink of tea for a chaser.

"Hard, same as always," Ella replied good-naturedly. "I swear, I don't think I'd know how to act if times wasn't hard." Then her voice became sad. "This latest dry spell, it's hurtin' lots of folks real bad. Some people done lost places they been

Hanging It on a Limb

on since Mr. Roosevelt was Pres'dent. The bank, it taken your granddaddy's place before he died."

"I heard," Maynard said, looking at the land beyond Luther's old wooden fence, land he had grown up on. "I aim to get it back."

"How?" Ella asked, frowning.

"Any way I can," Maynard said simply. And if he couldn't get it back, he thought, he would fix the banker, the son of a bitch, who took it. Fix him good.

Out in the yard, the young boy had turned around on the stump and was staring hard at Maynard. "Who's the boy?" Maynard asked Ella.

"Winona's," Ella said. "She was my youngest, remember? She went up to Detroit for a while; it was when you was away in the war, I think. One day she come back home carrying him in her belly. Soon's he born, why, some white man come in a big car and take her off. Three years later, she killed herself with drugs. The boy, he stayed here; didn't have no place else to go. We does the bes' we can for him, but he growing up moody and mean. Po' little devil ain't even got a proper name; gets called 'Detroit' 'cause that's where he started. Children in school tease him 'cause he's such a funny color."

Everybody's got problems, Maynard thought. He finished his iced tea and stood up. "I got to get going, Luther. I come by to tell you I was glad you was there when they buried my granddaddy. The prison people said I could go to the funeral, but I'd have had to wear cuffs and a waist chain. I wasn't going to say goodbye to my granddaddy with chains on. But I was right proud that you was there."

A single tear ran out of one of Luther's pitiful eyes and, still humming, he nodded his head very slowly.

When Maynard left the porch and crossed the yard, the boy, Detroit, turned away and would not look at him.

Hardhead, Maynard thought. Probably end up where I just came from.

Uptown in Elmo, Maynard drove once around the square and parked in front of the bank. Walking into its air-conditioned coolness, he stood for a moment as his eyes adjusted from bright sunlight to fluorescent. Presently his gaze settled on a man sitting behind a desk at the far rear of the room, surrounded by a walnut fence with a swinging gate. Maynard walked back, through the gate, and sat down. A sign on the man's desk read: EUGENE J. PHELPS, PRESIDENT.

"Well now," Maynard said, "you've come a long way since high school, Gene." A hardness edged into his tone. "You the one who took my granddaddy's place?"

"I hope you're not here looking for trouble, Mayne," Phelps said. A man with almost no chin, he was the same age as Maynard, but looked much younger; nicely tanned, his hair styled, nails manicured, his shirt was crisp, no wrinkles, not even any circles of sweat under the arms. Maynard, in his prison dress-outs and convict haircut, a jailhouse tattoo on one arm, nicotine stains on his fingers, could have been ten years older.

"I ain't looking for trouble," Maynard said. "I just want to find out how to get my granddaddy's place back."

"There's no way," the banker told him. "That place was foreclosed on for non-payment of a federal bank land loan. The property was lawfully auctioned and sold."

"Who bought it?"

"A land broker over in Savannah. But he doesn't have it anymore; he sold it to somebody else."

"Who?"

"Some investment company. Matsuo or something, over in Japan."

"Japan? What the hell," Maynard asked incredulously, "does anybody in Japan want with my granddaddy's place?"

"I wouldn't know," declared Phelps. "Those groups buy a lot of land and more often than not just let it lay. I think it gives them some kind of trade rights if they own property over here."

Maynard leaned forward tensely. "My granddaddy's daddy bought that land a hunnerd goddamn years ago. It ain't right for you to sell it to foreigners!"

"We sell it to the highest bidder, Mayne," the banker defended. "The Federal Farm Bank requires that. They even tell us when to foreclose. It's not *me*, Mayne; it's not even this bank; it's the government."

One of Maynard's calves jerked spastically as anger rippled his body. He had come back to Elmo with the intent of getting back his granddaddy's farm or shooting the banker that had taken it. Now he not only found that the banker was an old classmate of his, but apparently wasn't even to blame—not personally anyway. Who in the hell did that leave to shoot? The government?

Maynard sat back, sighing wearily. "When I come back from Vietnam, my granddaddy was so deep in debt on his farm that he almost lost it then. But I helped him out. I got him twenty thousand dollars to pay off everything and make a down payment on a new John Deere sidehill combine so's he could put in a crop on the slopes along with the flats. I figured all he needed was a fresh start, a new season—"

"Mayne, I know you thought at the time that you were doing right," Gene Phelps said quietly. "But holding up that fancy jewelry store in Atlanta and getting yourself put away for six years—well, maybe your granddaddy would have been better off if you'd just stayed on the farm and helped him."

Maynard shook his head. "I couldn't do that. I was all

strung out from those last fourteen months in Vietnam; then the Saigon evacuation, seeing all them people left behind, knowing what was gonna happen to them. And I brought back a drug habit I had to get shed of, too. There wasn't no way I could have turned into a peaceful dirt farmer overnight. I helped my granddaddy the only way I knew how."

"Look, Mayne," Phelps reasoned, "even if you could get the place back now, you wouldn't keep it; you'd just turn around and sell it yourself—"

"I wouldn't sell it," Maynard contradicted, shaking his head. "I'd give it to Luther Bates."

"Old blind Luther? What in the devil would you give land to that old colored man for?"

"He was my granddaddy's friend," Maynard replied simply. "He could get somebody to sharecrop it for him; might make his last days a little better for him."

"Well, it's a moot point anyhow," the banker said. "It's all over and done with." He drummed his fingers on the desktop. "Anything else you want to know?"

"I reckon not," Maynard said, rising. Phelps rose also and walked to the door with him.

"Now, listen, Maynard, if there's any way I can he'p you out, I want you to let me know. I mean it now, hear? We never were the best of friends, but we did play high school football together and all. 'Member those days? Boy, we were something, weren't we?"

"Yeah, we were," Maynard said. "It don't seem real, hardly. Seems more like a movie I once saw." His expression turned curious. "How's Nadine?"

"Fine, just fine, good as can be," Phelps said, a little too quickly, coloring slightly. "We've got two little ones now: a boy and a girl."

"Congratulations," Maynard said, taking care to keep his

tone neutral. The way Nadine had once performed in the back seat of his old Chevy, he was surprised they didn't have a dozen. That girl sure had liked it at seventeen. She had a little clover-like birthmark in the most peculiar place he had ever seen—

Outside the bank, the two men said goodbye and Maynard walked toward Buster's Cafe on the corner. Over his shoulder he noticed Gene Phelps crossing to the courthouse in the center of the square. Maynard grunted softly; the sheriff's office was in the courthouse. He guessed Gene was on his way to do his civic duty and let the sheriff know that an ex-convict was on the loose in Elmo. Two-faced bastard, he thought contemptuously.

Because it was too early for the supper trade, Buster's Cafe was nearly devoid of customers. Two ceiling fans moved the hot, grease-smelling air around while Buster, a big-bellied man whose soiled apron seemed to be holding up his stomach, sat reading a St. James bible and occasionally reaching out with a swatter to kill an unsuspecting fly.

"Hey, Bus," said Maynard.

"Well, lookee here," Buster responded with a smile. He struck out a fat hand to shake. "How you doing, boy? You didn't come in here to rob me, I hope; I ain't even made my overhead this week." Suddenly his fleshy face sank into sadness. "I sure am sorry about your granddaddy, Mayne."

"Well, he was an old man," Maynard said resignedly. "I just wish his last year had been better. Wish he could have died on his own place."

"Ain't that the truth. Want something to eat? I made okra soup this morning."

"Just some coffee, Bus." Maynard bobbed his chin at the bible. "You get religion?"

"Not exactly," Buster replied, drawing a cup of coffee.

"I've decided to become a television evangelist; you know, like Jimmy Swaggart and Jim Bakker and them. I'm tired of being a fry cook, even if it is in my own cafe. Way I look at it, I can prob'ly put on as good a show as them old boys does, and the way they've messed up lately, why, hell, there must be all kinds of good people just waitin' for somebody new to contribute to. But I don't want to be just another pretty face, know what I mean? I want to be the real thing. That's why I'm studying the good book. I might take singing lessons too." He put the cup of coffee in front of Maynard.

As Buster had been talking, Maynard noticed a Vietnamese woman come in from the kitchen carrying a tray of clean glasses which she proceeded to line up on a shelf behind the counter. Maynard raised his eyebrows inquisitively.

" 'Member Dewey Kidder?" Buster asked, lowering his voice to a confidential tone. "He was a year ahead of us in high school. 'Member he used to sleep in class a lot and ever'body said he'd never amount to nothing. Well, they was right; he's an accountant over in Valdosta. 'Fore he turned bad, though, he married this here little Vietnamese gal and brought her back from 'Nam. Settled down in a real good job pumping gas at Junior Munsell's Texaco station. Then along come this freckle-faced, redheaded little gal from Valdosta who decided that old Dewey was just the man of her dreams. Make a long story short, he left his Vietnamese wife, moved to Valdosta with Freckles, and her daddy sent the worthless hound to college so he could join the old man's accounting firm."

"So how'd you end up with the slant?" Maynard asked. A frown clouded Buster's face.

"Her name's Lan, Maynard. And I ain't 'ended up' with her, not like you think. I felt sorry for her, is all. Left all alone in a strange country, with strange people. So I give her a job an' I let her fix up a room out back to live in. Oh, I know what people in town think; every peckerwood I know gives me the old sly wink and stupid grin. But I don't care; I helped her when nobody else would." Buster looked away, his frown becoming a scowl. "I'd be obliged if you wouldn't call her a 'slant.' "

"Sure. I'm sorry, Bus. I didn't mean nothing by it. Just habit."

Buster shrugged and was silent for a moment, then he asked, "Want to meet her?"

It caught Maynard by surprise. "Uh—yeah. Okay."

"Lan, come here a minute," Buster called.

She left the glasses and hurried over, a thin, wafer of a woman with high, wide cheekbones and eyes as dark as ripe plums. She had an overbite that made her upper lip wider than the lower; narrow, square shoulders; almost no breasts that Maynard could see.

"Lan, this here's Mayne, my buddy," Buster introduced.

Maynard greeted her in Vietnamese, which seemed almost to embarrass her. "I am please you to meet," she replied in practiced but imperfect English.

A couple of truck drivers came in and Buster went to wait on them. Lan started to go away, but Maynard quickly made conversation. "Do you like it here in Elmo?"

"Sometime," she said, shrugging self-consciously. "Some people very nice. Some people not so nice."

"Buster's one of the nice ones, huh?"

"Oh, yes. Buster, he very best. Buster good man like I think American husband be. But I wrong."

"Yeah, well," Maynard said quietly, "being wrong's about the easiest thing anybody can do." Lan smiled briefly and again started to go, but Maynard took a quick gulp of coffee and pushed the cup toward her, saying, "Could I get this warmed up, please?"

When Lan brought the freshly filled cup back, it was she who continued the conversation. "I never see you in here before. You not live in Elmo?"

"I use to," Maynard said. He added wryly, "I been living up in north Georgia, learning a trade."

"Oh, to learn trade is good. What trade?"

"Uh, broom-making," he half mumbled.

"Broom making?"

"Uh, yeah. The state's got this broom-making plant up in—up north. I been working there, learning to make brooms and brushes and things."

"Ah," she said, nodding her head. "Is very good, state teach you good trade. State very kind."

"Yeah, very kind."

When Buster walked back up, Lan excused herself and returned to her work. "Nice gal, ain't she?" Buster said.

"Real nice," Maynard replied.

"That Dewey's a real prick, dumping her like he did. Listen, 'fore I forget, I got your granddaddy's trunk back in my storeroom. He had it moved over here from the boarding house when he went in the hospital. I guess he knew he wouldn't be coming out." Buster opened the cash register drawer and fished a key from one of the wells. "Come on, I'll show you where it is."

In a room lined with shelves of big lard cans, sacks of beans, crates of onions, and jars of mustard, pickles, and other condiments, there stood in one corner an old Civil War trunk of faded oak with tarnished metal trim, held shut by a thick brass hasp through which an old Master lock had been attached. Maynard knelt next to the trunk and rubbed his fingertips gently over the aged surface. Buster handed him the key, saying, "I'll leave you alone to look at his things."

Buster left and Maynard unlocked the Master and raised the trunk lid. There was a tray section on top, divided into little compartments, its surface covered with peeling decorative paper. His eyes scanning the contents, Maynard's fingers moved from one article to the next: an old pair of bifocals in a metal snap case; an expired fishing license; a RE-ELECT ROOSEVELT pin; a rolled-up belt with an initialed buckle; a yellowed newspaper clipping that read: MAYNARD GETS 2 YEARS; and a variety of other things: buttons, old pipes, a jackknife, a tobacco can of fish hooks; some snapshots that were turning brown. Maynard looked at the photographs: one of his daddy, shot and killed in a card game when Maynard was four; his mother, who ran off with a married neighbor two years later; his grandmother, whom he had never known, but about whom his granddaddy had told many warm, often humorous stories; even a few photos of himself and his granddaddy, taken during the years his granddaddy had raised him.

Beneath the tray, there was mostly old clothes and a few things that would not fit in the tray; two rifles, broken down, their stocks and barrels carefully wrapped; a ten-inch hunting knife in a sheath; a Colt's revolver with a six-inch barrel and bone grips; and a few boxes of cartridges. Taking the revolver from its nest in the layered clothing, Maynard hefted it for balance. The old six-shooter would have come in handy if he had found anyone to blame for taking his granddaddy's land and making the old man live his last year in a boarding house. But there was no one to blame; you couldn't shoot the government. Putting the pistol back, Maynard replaced the tray and locked the trunk.

Back out in the cafe, he asked Buster, "Okay if I leave the trunk here until I decide what to do?"

"Hell, yes." Buster scratched his head. "Funny, ain't it,

how a man's life can last as long as your granddaddy's did and still come down to one trunk full at the end. I guess that was all the bank left him. Old Gene Phelps don't miss much when he's selling to hisself."

Something pinched Maynard's brain. "What do you mean?"

"He's got hisself a land brokering business over in Savannah. It's not in his name, of course, but ever'body knows it's his. Anytime he forecloses on a farm, he turns around and buys it hisself through his brokering company by bidding a few hundred dollars more than anybody else. Then he re-sells the land at a big profit, usually to some Japanese buyer. Won't be many years, the U.S. is gonna *belong* to Japan."

"Are you sure?" Maynard asked. "About the Savannah business?"

"Positive. His cousin runs the place, but old Gene, he's got ninety percent of the stock. 'Course, it's in Nadine's name. Jerry Hickman's wife works in the Savannah business license department; she looked it up one time."

Another customer came in and Buster left Maynard alone at the counter. Maynard stared for a long moment at the black circle of coffee in his cup, then rose and returned to the back room and unlocked the trunk again.

He got out the pistol and loaded it.

It was just past dusk when Maynard slipped out of the woods behind Gene Phelps's house and moved quietly up to the open kitchen windows. Two black women were preparing supper, one slicing potatoes, one breading pork chops. A little girl was playing on the floor; she looked like Nadine except that she had no chin like Gene.

Maynard looked around. The house was in the middle of several acres, surrounded by trees, with no neighbor in sight.

Moving on, Maynard went around the side of the house and checked the open windows there until he found Gene. He was with Nadine. They were in a large bedroom, Gene lying on a king-size bed with his shoes off, reading a newspaper; Nadine, in her slip, was sitting at a vanity applying makeup. Drawing the pistol from his waistband, Maynard moved a few feet away, carefully cocked the hammer, then stepped back to the window. There he hesitated; he did not want to shoot Gene with Nadine in the room. He decided to wait a few minutes and see if they separated.

As Maynard stood there, the shadows around him deepening, he began to listen to the conversation in the bedroom.

"Just how long do you think I'm going to put up with this?" Nadine asked in a voice that sounded flinty. It was not the same throaty, backseat voice that Maynard remembered.

"Put up with what?" Gene asked disinterestedly.

"You know damn well what!" she snapped, turning on the vanity seat. She had gained weight, Maynard noticed. The tight little cheerleader body had become fleshy.

"Nadine, I've told you a hundred times," Gene said irritably, lowering the newspaper, "it is all over between Nancy Sue and me. I have *fired* the girl. What else do you want me to do: have her murdered?"

"I'm not talking about Nancy Sue," Nadine spat. "I'm talking about that slut you've got working for you in the Savannah office. What's her name—Dawny or Tawny—?"

"Fawny."

"Fawny. Isn't that cute? I just love all these pretty little names that young girls have these days. Fawny and Heather and Cindy and Tish. Do you realize how stupid those name are going to be when those girls get old? I mean *really* old: seventy, eighty. Can you picture a little old lady in some nursing home named Cindy? Or Heather?" She gave her husband a withering look. " 'Course, we both know it's not their names that interest you, don't we, sugar?"

"Now listen here, Nadine—"

"No, you listen to me, Gene Phelps! I have had it with your playing around! You are not going to make me the laughing-stock of this county!"

Just then the bedroom door opened and a little boy came in. "Mommy, why are you yelling at daddy?" he asked. Maynard studied the boy. He looked exactly like Gene had looked in the second grade. No chin.

"Mommy and daddy were just playing a game, sweetheart. You run along now and have Nettie get you ready for supper."

After the boy left, Gene sat up on the side of the bed, letting the newspaper drop to the floor. "It appears to me, Nadine, that it's a little late to begin worrying about your reputation in the county. If I had known all the things I later found out, we wouldn't be married in the first place, much less have kids."

"What do you mean by that?" she demanded, one stockinged foot beginning to tap nervously.

"I mean we already had the boy and you were pregnant with the girl when Bill Pete Wilkins got drunk one night over at the VFW club, forgot who he was drinking with, and told me all about the good times you had while I was away at college."

"You going to believe a lying drunk like Bill Pete Wilkins?" Nadine scoffed.

"He knows about your birthmark, honey." Gene said dryly. "And he's not the only one who knows." Picking up his shoes, he walked to the bedroom door. "Oh, before I forget," he added, "I have to spend the weekend in Savannah. Business." He walked out of the room.

Hanging It on a Limb

Maynard quickly moved from window to window on that side of the house to see where Gene was going. He could not find him in any of the rooms. Keeping to the shadows, holding the cocked pistol away from his body, he tried the opposite side of the house. Only the children's rooms were over there. Trotting to the kitchen again, he saw that Gene had not gone there. Could there be, he wondered, an interior room that had no windows? A study, maybe, or an office? Puzzled, sweating, the gun in his hand seeming to become heavier and heavier, Maynard made a complete circuit of the house again. When he got back to the bedroom window, he heard Nadine talking again and thought Gene had gone back in there. But when he looked in, he saw that she was just on the phone. He started to go on past, but her words stopped him.

"I've decided to file for divorce, Clarence. Gene and I have reached the point of total incompatibility. Naturally I want your law firm to handle it for me. Virginia and I have been such good friends for so long, I wouldn't think of using anyone else but her charming husband. Besides, I've already told you about the stock I hold in the land brokering firm; two things I intend to get out of this divorce are custody of my children and that stock. I know you told me there might be some conflict of interest charges against Gene once the stock comes to light, but I can't help that; it's his worry. Oh, Clarence, shame on me, I haven't even asked if Virginia is feeling any better. How is she, dear?"

As Maynard waited while Nadine listened on the telephone, he suddenly saw a light come on in a room near the other end of the house. He started to move toward it but Nadine began speaking again and her words held him there.

"I'm so sorry to hear that, Clarence. Maybe it's early menopause or something. Of course, it's doubly distressing to me because I know what a vigorous man you are—what?—

why certainly I remember, Clarence, don't be silly." After another pause, she said, "A drink and dinner? Just to discuss my case, you mean? How thoughtful of you not to make me come to your office. Listen, Gene will be in Savannah all weekend—"

Same old Nadine, Maynard thought. He moved in a crouch down to the other lighted window. Looking in, he saw that it was a small, comfortably furnished study, and that Gene had settled into a big leather recliner with a drink in one hand and a television remote control in the other.

Changing the gun to his left hand, Maynard wiped his right on the leg of his trousers. His palm and trigger finger dry, he took half a step back and balanced the heel of his hand and the gun handle on the window sill. Payback time, Mr. Banker, he thought, wetting his lips, swallowing—

He stood there for a full minute without firing.

Nadine's words ricocheted in slow motion off the inside of his skull. Divorce—conflict of interest—custody of the children. It would be a shame, Maynard thought, to deprive Gene Phelps of all the misery Nadine was planning for him.

Maynard lowered the gun. Staring through the window he thought: *You're gonna pay in a lot of ways for what you done.*

A lot of ways worse than a bullet.

Moving away from the house, into the darkness, Maynard uncocked the gun.

Buster's Cafe was closed by the time Maynard got back to town. He parked behind it and knocked on the back door until Lan finally came to see who it was.

"I'd like to get that trunk Buster let me leave here," he said.

She let him in and he started dragging the trunk out of the storeroom. Halfway through the kitchen, he paused and looked thoughtfully at her.

"Listen, Lan, I'm on my way down to a little town in the Florida panhandle that has a brush manufacturing plant that hires—well, that hires people like me—"

"Like you?" she asked, puzzled. "How like you?"

"People who know how to make brooms and stuff," he said, unable to muster the courage at that moment to tell her the ex-convict part of it. Later, perhaps, if anything developed between them. "Anyway, what I was thinking, if you'd like to get out of Elmo and make a new start, why, you could come along with me—?"

"You want me be your woman?" she asked candidly.

"Well, I don't know," Maynard hedged. "Maybe. I mean, if you wanted to. You wouldn't have to. But if we get to liking one another—"

"Okay," she agreed. "Sound good to me. I go call Buster."

"Yeah, you do that. Go call Buster." He could not help being a little surprised at how quickly the arrangement had been consummated.

He finished dragging the old trunk out and got it into the car. Presently Lan came out carrying a cheap little suitcase. "Buster say if you not treat me good, he come to Florida and kick you in ass."

"He prob'ly would too," Maynard laughed.

They drove a little ways out of town and then Maynard suddenly pulled over and stared at the lights of a house back off the road. Presently he turned off the engine.

"I just want to stop here a minute," he told her.

Gravel crunched under his shoes as he left the car and hurried toward the lights. Waiting alone in the darkness, Lan shivered slightly. There was a round clock on the dashboard but she was not certain it was working. He said he was just going to stop for a minute. The clock wasn't working, she was sure of it. She decided to count to sixty; that would be a minute. She began.

When she got to sixty, he still was not back. Maybe she had counted too fast. She counted again. When she finished this time, she began to feel afraid. She got quietly out of the car and looked hard toward the lights of the house. She had almost made up her mind to walk toward the lights, when she heard the crunch of gravel again.

Maynard emerged from the shadows. There was a young boy with him, carrying a bundle of clothes.

"This here's Detroit," Maynard said. "He's going with us."

They all got into the car and drove away.

After they had gone a couple of miles, Detroit asked, "Is this like hanging it on a limb? Getting away from someplace?"

"That's exactly what it is," Maynard replied quietly. "And maybe it's the last time any of us will ever have to do it,"

When they got to the highway, Maynard turned south toward Florida.

The title of this story tells you that the scene is the "Big Easy" again—New Orleans.

And in the first two sentences you'll learn that there's another hardhead who just got out of another penitentiary, and you'll know he's going to find some problems dealing with life on the outside.

Maybe he'll be lucky like "Maynard" in HANGING IT ON A LIMB *and find people like the Vietnamese woman "Lan" and the boy called "Detroit" to help him change his life.*

Or maybe his luck will run out like it did for "Tree O'Hara" when he trusted the woman named "Vi" in WILD THINGS.

For certain, this hardhead has no idea that he's about to encounter a kid without a playground, a blonde girl half his age, a burglar-turned-preacher, and a robbery getaway that goes from bad to worse . . .

New Orleans Getaway

Moss Lemoyne arrived in New Orleans on the five-thirty bus from St. Francisville. He had been discharged from Angola, the state penitentiary, at eleven o'clock that morning. His face reflected the nine years he had served: a slight squint and a permanent tan from the hot sun of the fields; palms that were shiny from the wooden handle of his hoe; a habit of barely moving his lips when he spoke. He was forty-four, but his life had stopped at thirty-five. He had lost nearly a decade, and inside him somewhere was a nagging urge to catch up.

Outside the bus station, a cab driver looked him up and down, and said, "Taxi, bud?"

Moss shook his head. "I'll walk. Canal Street still in the same place?"

"Unless they've moved it since breakfast, it is."

Moss tucked his extra clothes and shaving gear, which were wrapped in a brown paper parcel, under one arm and walked the two blocks to Canal Street. It was bustling, just as he remembered it: people, cars, trucks, trolleys—everything and everybody moving almost in a frenzy. Life in the fast lane, Moss thought. It was a saying he had heard from some young kid, a new fish who had come into the walls a while back. Feeling suddenly dizzy, Moss stepped into a doorway and stood very still. He had skipped breakfast that morning: too excited about getting out; then the bus ride; now all this noise and movement on Canal Street. Better slow down, pard, he told himself. Get yourself to Coley's place and get something to eat.

Coley's Cafe was on a narrow, dingy little side street just a block from the river. Moss walked past it first and went down to the edge of the wharf to look at the Big Muddy—the Mississippi River. The Beauregard, a tourist paddle boat, was just coming in to anchor. Upriver, near the Ponchartrain Bridge, two rusty freighters were passing each other. Across the water was Gretna, the little town where Moss had grown up. He had three brothers and three sisters, and not one of them was still in Louisiana. They were spread out all over the country now, some of them he didn't even know where. Moss shook his head briefly. Where the hell does life go? he wondered.

He walked back to Coley's and went in. It was a seedy little joint, long and narrow like a boxcar, with all counter stools, no booths. The place smelled of grease and fried onions and cold hushpuppies, but to Moss it still smelled better than prison. There were only two customers at the counter, both bums, nursing coffee. Coley was on a high stool next to the cash register, reading a racing form, picking his teeth with a toothpick. He had one leg, his right, stuck out straight alongside the stool. It was a wooden leg. Coley had lost it twenty years earlier after being shot in a bank robbery. He'd hidden out on a friend's farm, refusing to have a doctor called, and gangrene had set in. Coley was the only man on record to serve a full term for bank robbery in Leavenworth with a wooden leg.

"Hey, Coley," Moss said quietly, taking a stool across from him.

"Moss! Hey, man!" Coley's face turned on like a new bulb. He folded the scratch sheet, tossed the toothpick on the floor, and stuck out his hand. "You're looking good, boy, real good. Healthy."

"Home-grown vegetables," Moss said. Angola, the largest prison compound in the country, grew everything its prisoners ate. Some said it was the best prison food anyplace.

"They cut you loose this morning?" Coley asked. Moss nodded. "Old Burley still in charge of the dressing-out clothes?" Moss nodded again. Old Burley was a black man who had been in Angola for fifty-two years, since he was fourteen. He no longer believed there was an outside world; he thought it was all made up. "I bet he's seen a million guys get out," Coley said.

"At least," Moss agreed.

"You hungry?"

"Starving."

"Skipped breakfast, huh? Want anything special?"

"Anything'll do, with lots of milk."

Coley limped back to the kitchen and spoke to his fry cook. When he came back, he studied Moss Lemoyne for a moment, then asked, "What else you need?"

"A room for a couple of nights," Moss told him.

"Got one right upstairs. It ain't fancy but the rent's free."

"And I want to find Keene Summers," Moss said.

"Keene? Hell, that's easy. He's preaching now, you know."

"Preaching?"

"Yeah. You knew his daddy was a preacher. Well, when his daddy passed, as the blacks say, all them people in the old man's congregation got together and made Keene their preacher."

"But Keene's a burglar," Moss said, staring at Coley.

Coley shook his head. "Preacher."

A thin young girl with ruler-straight blonde hair entered the cafe, said "Hi, Mr. Coley," and went on back to the kitchen.

"Who's that?" Moss asked.

"My night girl. Runs the place from six 'til midnight."

"Little young for that kind of responsibility, ain't she?"

Coley shrugged. "Ain't much business at night. Just stragglers mostly. Coffee-and-pie types with no place to go, killing time. She needed a job. Anyway, she says she's twenty."

Moss grunted. "She's twenty, I'm honest."

Coley stared thoughtfully at him. "You could be, you know," he said quietly.

"Could be what? Honest?"

"Sure. It ain't so bad. Look at me, I'm doing okay. I been honest, or at least pretty near honest, for six years now."

"With you it's different. You went straight because—well—"

"Because of my leg, go ahead and say it. But you're wrong. I didn't turn honest because of my leg; I turned honest because of my head," Coley tapped his temple. "I got smart, Moss, I wised up. You could too."

"Save it," Moss said without rancor. "Thought you said it was Keene doing the preaching. How about that room now? I'll take my supper with me."

"Sure."

Moss followed the limping man back to the kitchen where the cook had just set a large platter of steak, fries, and onion rings on the service counter.

"Put a cover over that and put it on a tray with a pitcher of milk," Coley told him. "Jaysie," he said to the blonde girl, "show my friend to that spare room upstairs."

Jaysie carried the supper tray and led Moss up a flight of inside back stairs to a windowless room with a slanted ceiling. In the room was a cot, a round wooden table with two straight chairs, a dresser with a cracked mirror, and a small fan.

"The fan's for when it gets too hot," Jaysie said.

"Glad you told me that," Moss replied dryly.

She blushed. "Bathroom's that door we passed at the top of the stairs." She put the tray on the table and started to leave.

"What kind of a name is Jaysie?" Moss asked.

"Oh, it's not a name, really," she said, pausing at the door. "What it really stands for is my initials: J. C. Janie Carol."

Moss walked over to her. "How old are you, Janie Carol?"

"I'm twenty," she replied, shifting her eyes. She again started to leave and Moss caught hold of her wrist.

"How old?"

"I said I was twenty."

He tightened his grip. "Try again."

"All right! I'm seventeen! Let go!"

Moss turned her loose and fixed her in a flat stare. "Coley is a good friend of mine. I don't want to see him get in any dutch over some runaway kid, understand me?"

"How'd you know I was a runaway?" she asked, almost indignantly.

"Lucky guess," Moss replied in the same dry tone he had used earlier. "Do you take my meaning about trouble for Coley?"

"I hear you," she said, half angry, half pouting. "But I wouldn't do nothing to hurt Mr. Coley. He's been good to me. 'Sides, I kind of feel sorry for him; I mean, him losing his leg in the war and all."

Moss managed to keep his expression straight. "He told you about that, did he?"

"Sure. Told me all about how he won all them medals and then lost his leg in Korea. He's a real hero."

"A real hero," Moss agreed.

After the girl left, Moss sat down and tried to control his laughter enough to eat.

The sign in front read:

DIXIE EZEKIEL BAPTIST CHURCH
REV. KEENE SUMMERS, PASTOR

As Moss stood looking at it, a skinny black boy, ten or eleven, came up with a homemade wooden box slung over one shoulder.

"Shine, mister?"

Moss looked down at the brown prison brogans he had been issued the previous day. Although new, they were state-made from reject-grade leather and were incapable of taking a shine. But the kid looked hungry.

"Sure," Moss said. He stepped over to a cypress tree in the grassless, worn-down church front yard and leaned against it.

New Orleans Getaway

The black kid got the shine box under one foot and went to work.

Next door to the church was a playground as barren as the yard: torn, limp volleyball net, bent basketball hoop, faded lines that had once been a shuffleboard court. "How come nobody's in the playground?" Moss asked the kid. The boy grunted scornfully.

"That playground ain't no good, man. Ain't got no 'quipment, so can't play no games. Need 'quipment to play games, you know."

The boy worked on Moss's shoes for twenty minutes, and when he finished they looked exactly like they had when he started.

"Fi'ty cents," the boy said, holding out his hand. Moss gave him a dollar and the kid pretended that he didn't have any change. Moss, knowing he was being worked, let him keep it all.

Inside the Dixie Ezekiel Church, Moss told a heavyset black cleaning woman that he wanted to see Pastor Summers. She led him to a small office in the rear of the building.

"Hey, Keene," Moss said to the handsome black man, ten years younger than himself, who sat behind a cluttered desk.

"Moss," Keene Summers said, quietly, almost matter-of-factly, as if he might have been expecting him. He got up, came around the desk, and embraced Moss. "Moss, my friend, it's good to see you, really very good. You certainly look fit."

"Home-grown vegetables," Moss said. "But then you know that yourself."

"I certainly do," Keene said, laughing at a joke which he knew to be on himself.

"I saw your name outside," said Moss. "Does your congregation know it used to have a number after it?"

"Yes, of course," Keene said. He returned to his chair behind the desk. "I grew up in this district, Moss. Everybody knows I took a fall for burglary when I was twenty-one. They all know I was sent to the adult reformatory; that I was a bad dude there and after one year got thrown behind the walls at Angola. And they know I did seven years there."

Moss raised his eyebrows. "They still let you be their pastor?"

"Not 'let,' Moss; they *insisted*. You see, my granddaddy founded Dixie Ezekiel in 1899. My daddy was pastor here for over thirty years. When Daddy passed, the church board came to me and asked me to take over. I had assisted Daddy for about five years, since I got out of prison. He had ordained me when he found out he had cancer. I tried to get out of it; Lord knows, I didn't feel any calling to it. But the board, the entire congregation, insisted. They wanted me and they finally got me."

Moss smiled. "Nice work for a burglar."

Summers gazed at Moss but did not reply to the comment. Moss let him gaze for a full minute, then rose and removed his coat. "Warm in here," he said. Sitting back down, he carefully, deliberately, rolled up his shirt sleeves. When he got the right one rolled up, it revealed on his forearm an ugly, bluish, puffy nine-inch scar that had obviously once been a terrible wound.

Keene Summers looked at the scar, smiled tolerantly, and said, "What is it you want, Moss?"

"I remember the day I got this," Moss said running a fingertip along the scar. "We were all in the noon chow line. You had transferred in from the reformatory a week earlier; you were right ahead of me in line but we didn't know each other. All of a sudden, I heard the guy behind me whisper, 'Shank!' real scared like. I looked around and here's this big dude bearing down with a shank that had to be one of the best prison-made knives I ever seen: made out of melted toothbrush handles, molded about six inches long, both edges and the point sharpened like a razor on the cement floor. Beautiful. Anyway, I see this dude bearing down, and I've got no idea that he's the brother of a cat you had a run-in with in the reformatory. All's I know is that he's getting ready to shove his Pepsodent shrank into the side of your neck. I don't like to see nobody get it when they're not looking, so I threw up my arm to try to knock the shank out of his hand. Instead, I took the blade myself. Ripped my whole arm open. Took four months to heal." Moss flexed his bicep. "Never did get a hundred percent use of it back; doc says about ninety percent. And a funny thing: it aches every time the weather's damp. Like arthritis."

Keene sat forward and put his hands together on the desk. "I know you probably saved my life, Moss. I've always been grateful to you for it. But I repeat, what do you want?"

"You said you owed me that day. You said anything, anytime. Remember?"

"I do."

"Well, this is the time, and here's the thing: I need a partner. For a vault job up in Baton Rouge."

"I'm a minister now, Moss," said Keene. "You can't be serious."

"I'm dead serious, man," Moss assured him. "Look, I think it's jake that you got your daddy's church and all; I'm glad you've got a good set-up. But I *ain't* got one. I'm forty-four years old, man. I've done two stretches totaling fifteen years on the inside. I got no family, no trade, no prospects, and no future."

"But you've got something a lot of men *never* get, Moss: a fresh start." Keene's voice had turned eager. "Look, you don't need a vault job. Let me help you find a *real* job, an honest job. You're not too old to make a new start."

"Right. I'm going to make a new start, my friend, but it's not gonna be at the bottom of the ladder. I figure if I get me a nice stake, I can buy into some little business somewhere. I been keeping up on things by reading business magazines; I figure something like videotape rentals or electronic games would have a good future. But I need a stake first." He fixed Keene in a flat gaze. "And I need a good partner. Somebody I can depend on. Somebody who owes me."

Keene Summers sighed heavily and sat back in his chair. His glance fell on Moss's scarred arm again. He imagined that scar along the side of his own face—which is where it would probably be if the knife hadn't killed him. Yeah, he owed Moss, all right. But a *vault job?* Did he owe him that much?

"Moss, I don't know if I'd be any good on a job anymore," Keene said quietly. "I've been straight for so long that I—well, I'm not sure I'd hold up well."

"On this job you'd hold up," Moss assured him. "It's a hot car operation up in Baton Rouge. Keeps big money on hand to pay for its merchandise. The job's a snap. And your end will probably be twenty-five or thirty thousand. That kind of dough," he added pointedly, "would go a long way toward fixing up that playground of yours that don't seem to be attracting too many kids."

Keene smiled an almost embarrassed smile. "We are a poor church, Moss," he admitted. "But if I had twenty-five or thirty thousand dollars, I wouldn't put it into the playground. There's another, much more important project that would take priority over the playground. It's a day care center that we've been trying to get going. We're so poor around here, and wages are so low in the black community in general, that in most families the wife has to work just to make ends meet. But she needs someplace reliable to leave her children; a place that won't charge her so much that it's not worth her while to work. That's where our church comes in: we're trying to set up a free day care center. But it takes money: for cribs, youth beds, food, games, a place to put it all in, salaries for people to run it." Keene sighed almost resignedly. "You're right, Moss, twenty-five or thirty thousand dollars *would* go a long way." The young black man drummed the fingertips of one hand soundlessly on the desktop. After an awkward moment, he asked, "Where, uh—where did you get the vault job?"

"Contracted it," Moss replied. "From Henry Palmetto." Keene's eyebrows raised and an immediate look of interest spread over his face—as Moss had known it would. Henry Palmetto was a master planner of burglaries, considered to be one of the best case-men in the business. Once an intimate of Willie Sutton, he was reputed to have set up more than a hundred of the most successful burglaries in the country, and he had never been caught for any of them. He was in prison today only because of his involvement with an unfaithful woman, whom he had been obliged to kill. From his cell where he was serving life, he continued to set up burglaries of all sizes for a percentage of the take.

"Tell me about the job," Keene said.

"Like I mentioned," said Moss, "it's a front for a hot car ring up in Baton Rouge. From the outside it looks like an ordinary used car lot; they even keep a few dozen legitimate sale cars just to make it look good. And they actually sell some of them. But the big money is in stolen cars. They specialize in American-made luxury stuff: Coupe de Villes, Continentals, Rivieras, Tornados. The cars are grabbed in other states, Louisiana plates put on them and driven back to Baton

Rouge. The car lot has a garage and paint shop behind it. Six hours after they get a hot car, they have it completely painted a new color, have different seats in it, a new serial number burned into the engine block, and a forged Louisiana title and registration fixed up for it. Then they drive them over to Texas, run them across the border into Mexico, and sell them for six or eight grand apiece. They handle a dozen cars a week and take in seventy to ninety thousand. Palmetto says they've been operating without a hitch for a long time and never been touched. They're fat, lazy, and ripe."

"What's the layout?" Keene asked.

"The car lot office is a one-story block wall building in the middle of the lot. Tar-and-asbestos roof. Alarm system is a light-and-buzzer deal wired to the doors and windows only; it's connected to a security firm downtown. The vault is a Warnecke triple-plate, triple-tumbler model; it'll peel or burn, whatever. There's a night watchman on the premises from the time the lot closes until it gets light the next morning. This time of year he leaves about six A.M. Palmetto says the best time to do it is between then and nine in the morning when they open. The best day is Monday, because the weekend car sales money will be there too."

"What's Palmetto's end?"

"Fifteen percent of what's in the vault. We pay our own expenses."

Keene Summers rose and walked to the office's single window. Standing with his hands clasped behind his back, he gazed out at the run-down, deserted playground, wondering where all the kids were who should have been playing there. Beyond the playground, he studied a shabby, abandoned house that had been deeded to Dixie Ezekiel Church, and which he hoped could be refurbished into a day care center. So much to be done, he mused, and so little time, so little money. This vault job almost seemed like a gift from heaven; a gift which would permit him to free himself of his obligation to Moss Lemoyne, while at the same time securing enough money to get started on the day care center. And it wouldn't be like he was stealing from anyplace that mattered. After all, what was the place but a front for a hot car operation. Was stealing from people who steal really stealing? Couldn't one suppose that the Savior would forgive that kind of transgression?

Keene smiled at his own reflection in the window. Come on, boy, you know better than that, he chided himself. Go in on the vault job if you want to, but don't try to hustle the Lord for a partner. Maybe God will understand and maybe He won't: you'll never know until Judgment Day. Meanwhile, Keene concluded his thoughts, we need the day care center *now*.

Keene turned to Moss again. "I'll provide the car, the tarp, and the hand tools. You get the drill and the accessories. I think a Walsh 200-series drill ought to do it. Better get a dozen bits just in case. My Sunday night service concludes at nine; we'll leave for Baton Rouge right after." He put his hand out to Moss. "Deal?"

"Deal," said Moss, shaking hands.

That night, in his room above the cafe, Jaysie brought him a tray with his supper on it. "Can I ask you a question?" she said as he sat down to eat.

"I guess so."

"How old are you?"

"Old enough to be your daddy and then some," he replied.

"No, I mean it. How old are you, really?"

"Forty-four going on ninety. Don't you have work to do downstairs?"

"I'm on my break," she announced loftily. " 'Sides, there hasn't been a customer in the place for two hours. It's pouring rain out; if you had a window you'd know that. Can I sit down?"

"No."

Moss was in his undershirt and Jaysie saw his scarred arm. "Lordy, where'd you get that?" she asked in wonder. It was the worst scar she had ever seen.

"Korean War," said Moss. "I was in the same outfit Coley was in when he lost his leg. Will you beat it now and let me eat supper in peace?"

"If you'll tell me one thing first, I'll go," she said. "How'd you know so quick I was a runaway?"

Moss paused in his eating and looked steadily at her. Her pencil-thin body was almost as straight as her ironed blonde hair: she had practically no hips, no bust. Her collarbone stuck out above the scoop of her blouse, and her shoulder blades stuck out under it in back. Her arms looked too skinny to do anything heavy, yet Moss knew she was strong; he knew it from when he had grabbed her wrist that first day. He suspected that her legs, which were shapely and her best physical attribute, were also strong.

"Your eyes," he said in answer to her question. "There's a vacant, hollow look in them that says tomorrow's going to be exactly the same as today. All runaways have that look. And all junkies. And all convicts. All the losers."

"Well, *I'm* not a loser," she said defiantly. She met his direct eyes and immediately looked down. "At least not a permanent loser. I'll make it someday."

"Sure you will," Moss said without enthusiasm. "Someday." He resumed eating.

Jaysie stood looking at him for a long moment, watching him eat, watching him deliberately keep his eyes averted, purposely not looking at her anymore. Finally she grunted inwardly, wordlessly, and left him to the solitude of the lonely little room.

After supper, Moss went out again. He took a bus over to an area behind the St. Louis Cemetery, where a row of small garages and repair shops occupied the limited space beneath an elevated highway. The place he went in was Claude's Welding Shop. Claude was a rotund little man with constantly drooping eyelids that made him look sleepy or on something. Moss never could figure out which. From Claude, Moss bought on credit the Walsh 200-series drill he needed, and ten bits, which was all Claude had on hand. He also picked up two pairs of welding goggles to protect their eyes against flying slivers of metal; two pairs of moleskin gloves to absorb the sweat from their hands when they were drilling; and two pairs of engineer's coveralls to keep the steel dust off their street clothes. Claude packed everything neatly into a black canvas bag.

"You'll get your money Monday afternoon," Moss told the sleepy-eyed little welder.

"Yeah, okay, fine," said Claude, who reiterated everything he said. "Listen, I can order them two extra bits for you. I mean, if you want a dozen, I can get two more. I can order 'em for you, you know?"

"Ten will do," Moss said. "See you Monday."

"So long. Goodbye. See you," said Claude.

When Moss got back to the cafe, Coley was there with a tall redhead wearing spike heels and a coral pantsuit. Coley himself had on a white linen suit and open-collar navy shirt. When he saw Moss come in with the canvas bag, he moved over to intercept him at the back stairs.

"Been to see Claude, huh?" Coley said.

Moss nodded. "Who's the redhead?"

"Estelle Dumond. She dances down at the Burgundy Club; a specialty number. This is her night off. We been making it together for about a year now." He tapped his wooden leg. "She likes me 'cause I never take her dancing. She hates dancing. Like people who work in candy factories, you know. They never eat candy." Coley glanced down at the bag. "So everything's set, huh?"

"Yeah."

"Jeez, I wish I could talk you out of it, Mossy. I'd hate to see you fall and go back inside. You'd be old and gray time you got out again."

"A man's got to play it the only way he knows how, Coley. You understand that."

"I *used* to understand that," Coley said emphatically. "Not no more. Now I know a guy can break the mold if he wants to bad enough. I done it. Keene done it. You can do it too. Listen, I'll tell you what I'll do. Take that bag back to Claude and tell him you changed your mind. Then come to work for me. I need a new fry cook, for nights, to work with Jaysie. The guy I got is going to Miami to try to get back together with his ex-wife. Work for me a while, settle down, show me your head's on right, and then we'll sit down and talk about that little business of your own that you want: video tapes or games or whatever."

Moss's eyes narrowed knowingly. "Been talking to Keene, have you?"

Coley shrugged. "What's the diff? We're all friends, ain't we? Now getting back to this little business of yours, if the idea looks good, I'll borrow the dough and stake you. What do you say?"

Moss looked down at the floor so that Coley would not see how touched he was by the offer. "I appreciate what you're trying to do, Coley. Really. But I've got to go my own way. You understand that, don't you?"

Before Coley could answer, the redhead called to him from the front door. "Coley, honey, we're going to be late if you don't come on."

"Right there," Coley called back. "We're taking the supper cruise on the Beauregard," he explained to Moss. "Just like a couple of square tourists." For a moment then, the two men stood in awkward silence, both looking down at the floor. Finally Coley grinned and slapped him on the back. "Sure, I understand. Good luck, pal."

"Thanks," Moss said.

The cafe was closed Sunday night when Moss got ready to go meet Keene, so when he came downstairs he was surprised to find Jaysie sitting at the counter with an open book and a cup of coffee in front of her.

"Thought this was your night off," he said, putting the canvas bag on the floor and drawing a cup of coffee for himself.

"It is. But I like to study here 'cause it's quiet. The rooming house where I live is full of jazz musicians. They're always practicing. Makes it hard to concentrate."

Moss turned the book up to see its title. "Basic English," he read. "Where you studying that?"

"At Foster Continuation School. That's a school for people who never finished high school. I'm taking spelling and typing too. I don't intend to have that vacant look, as you call it, in my eyes forever. All of *my* tomorrow's am *not* going to be the same."

"Good for you," Moss said.

His voice had such a neutral tone that Jaysie was not sure whether he meant it or if he was just being sarcastic again.

She glanced down at the canvas bag. "You leaving?"

"Not tonight. But I will be soon. Probably tomorrow or the next day."

"Oh." She looked away.

Moss frowned. "You sound disappointed."

She shrugged. "It's just that Mr. Coley said that he was going to try to get you to be his night fry cook for a while. I guess you turned him down."

"Yeah, I did." Moss could not understand why he suddenly felt self-conscious. "I, uh, I've got other plans."

Jaysie turned to face him directly. "I hope whatever they are," she said firmly, "that they help *you* lose the vacant look in your own eyes. Because it is there, you know. You do have it, same as me."

Moss stared down into his circle of black coffee without replying. He could not deny it. He knew she was right. For weeks, months, years in prison, he had watched the look settle in his eyes, seen it daily in his prison-issue metal mirror—a dullness, a hollowness, an absence of anything hopeful—reflecting the knowledge that Friday would be like Thursday, Thursday like Wednesday, Wednesday like Tuesday, and all the days of his life were running together like the cells on a tier, an endless line, each the same as the one after it and the one before it.

He turned to Jaysie with a slight, sad smile. "You're right, kid. I'm a loser too."

"Then why don't you do like I'm doing?" she asked urgently. "Try to get out of your rut. Try to make things better for yourself." She put a hand on his arm. "Take the job Mr. Coley offered you. Please, Moss."

It was the first time she had called him by name. The first time he had heard any female voice speak his name in over nine years. For some reason it moved him. But not enough.

He patted the hand on his arm.

"I am going to try, Jaysie. But in my own way." He glanced up at a Dr. Pepper clock on the wall. "I've got to go."

Jaysie suddenly leaned forward and kissed him briefly on the lips. "I sometimes study very late," she said softly.

"Sorry," Moss said, "but I'll be out all night."

At the Dixie Ezekiel Baptist Church, Moss entered by the back door and waited in Keene's office. It was warm and the windows were open. Moss could hear Keene preaching at the Sunday night meeting—hear his voice loud and clear as he praised Jesus and challenged Satan, shouted the goodness of eternal salvation and warned of the tortures of eternal damnation—as he called for sinners to come forward and be saved, pleaded, cajoled, teased, and prodded them into coming forward to accept Jesus Christ as their savior. Keene's voice was powerful, moving, tenacious; it loomed above the "Amens!" and "Hallelujahs!" and "Yes, Brothers!" that mingled in with his fervent message. And when it was over, the organ began to play and all the voices merged as one to sing "Just a Closer Walk with Thee." It was the first song Moss had ever learned as a kid, growing up across the river in Gretna. The words came back to him now and he closed his eyes and sang them softly to himself:

> "Through this life of toil and snares,
> If I falter, Lord, who cares?
> Who for me my burden bears?
> None but Thee, dear Lord, none but Thee."

The old gospel song swept a rush of memories through Moss's head. He saw himself again as a little white boy stowing away on the ferry to cross over to New Orleans, there to wander the levees with other little boys, some white, some colored, listening to the Creole jazz bands play on street corners, begging food at the kitchen doors of the great houses on Royal Street, watching the fancy ladies from the Quarter strut along Bourbon Street with the pride of princesses. Life had been simple then. So very simple.

Moss was so caught up in his own thoughts that he didn't hear the music and praying end, did not know the Sunday night service was over until Keene came in and said, "Hey, Moss."

He opened his eyes then, the past back where it belonged. "Hey, Keene."

"Everything set?"

"Set," Moss confirmed.

Moss watched Keene empty his pockets and wallet of everything that could identify him. Like Moss, he would carry nothing in his pockets but a little money and the business card of a good lawyer. As Keene took things out of his wallet, Moss noticed a photo of a pretty young woman with an Afro, and a little girl with her hair braided in corn rows.

"Who's that?" he asked.

"My wife and daughter," Keene said.

Moss stared incredulously at him. "I didn't know you had a family."

"Sure. Little girl's four."

"Why didn't you say something?"

"What for? Would it have made any difference to you? I still owe you, Moss, whether I have a family or not."

"Yeah, but—"

"But nothing, man. Come on, let's hit the road."

They took three hours to drive to Baton Rouge, taking the back roads along the river, staying off the Interstate with its fast traffic and state police cars. They drove through little river settlements like Reserve, Romeville, Dutchtown, and Sunshine; smelled the smoky, dusky outdoor fires that the bayou people built nightly, summer and winter; smelled fish frying an hour after being pulled out of the Big Muddy; smelled the willows, the riverbanks, the okra and crawfish and greens being steamed for Cajun gumbo. And everywhere along the road there was music, all lonely, all soulful: a mournful harmonica, a blue guitar, a slow, lazy Jew's harp.

"Nothing ever changes down here, does it?" Moss said, more a statement than a question.

"Not hardly," Keene replied quietly.

They drove in silence for most of the trip, and got into Baton Rouge a little after midnight. Driving past the used car lot, they saw a light inside where the night watchman was probably sitting.

"What time's daylight, you reckon?" Keene asked.

"Five forty-two," Moss said. "I called the weather bureau long distance to find out."

They found an all-night chili joint and killed two hours there, eating a late supper, reading a discarded Sunday paper. Then they pulled onto a Holiday Inn lot, parked the car in a back corner, and slumped down in the seat to doze for a couple of hours.

At five-fifteen, they were again cruising the street that the used car lot was on. They watched daylight come slowly, dark to gray to light. The night watchman left at ten minutes to six. They waited until six to make sure he wouldn't pull the old trick of going around the block a couple of times. Then they parked behind the building, stood on top of the car, and scrambled onto the roof. Moss carried the canvas bag containing the drill, bits, and clothing; Keene handled the hand tools and the square folded tarpaulin with its rope and hardware.

It took them sixteen minutes to punch a hole in the roof and drop down into the office. Twelve minutes to twist screw hooks into facing walls and lash up the tarp to seal off their light and noise from the front. Four minutes to lay out their drill and bits, get into their coveralls, don gloves and goggles.

Then they were ready to drill. They took turns, one drilling while one watched the street. The drilling was hard, hot work. Sweat poured down their necks, laced their forearms, spread in a circle in the small of their backs. The Warnecke vault was one tough baby: steel on top of steel on top of steel. The first drill bit broke in four minutes, less than an eighth of an inch into the outer plate. The second one broke five minutes later; the third and fourth less than ten minutes after that. By the time they were halfway through the middle plate, they had broken three more. A total of seven dead bits.

"Good thing we got a dozen," Keene said, wiping the sweat from his face. "We'll probably need every one of them."

Talking the drill for his turn, Moss said nothing to Keene about having only ten bits. During his turn on the drill, he was very careful to keep the drill-nose as level-straight as possible.

Keene took the drill again when black slivers told them they had reached the bottom plate. Immediately he broke another bit biting into it.

"Take it easy, will you?" Moss said with an edge. "Slow down a little."

"I want to get out of here, my friend," Keene said. "Besides, we've got four bits left. No bottom plate can stand up to four Walsh bits."

Halfway through the bottom plate, Keene broke their ninth bit.

"I'll take it now," Moss said. Wetting his lips, he slugged

the last bit into the drill, took a deep breath and started to drill. He had a quarter of an inch of steel to get through. If he didn't make it, the job would go down the drain. He drilled slowly, carefully, for five minutes. Sweat, both from the effort and the tension, drenched his torso.

"Take a break, man," Keene said after five minutes. "Let me spell you again."

"I'm okay," Moss said. "Watch the street."

Keene went back to the edge of the tarp and resumed his scrutiny of the street. Several minutes later, Moss came over to him, shoulders slumped, but a look of relief in his eyes.

"We're through the bottom plate. Go punch the lock."

"All right!" Keene said happily.

They climbed back through the hole in the roof at twenty past eight with the canvas bag packed with sheaves of currency. The goggles, coveralls, tarp, and miscellaneous tools were left behind; only the drill, which had a traceable serial number, was brought back out. After they got in the car, they stripped off the moleskin gloves and tossed them on the ground next to the building.

"We've got forty, maybe forty-five minutes to get across the St. Gabriel bridge before the alarm's sounded and roadblocks go up," Moss said.

"You think they'll blow the whistle?" Keene asked.

"Sure they will. All they have to say is that we hit them for the week's car sales receipts. They'll probably call in the law just to get us caught. Then take care of us themselves later."

As they headed back south by way of the same bayou roads, Moss unzipped the canvas bag, tossed the drill on the back seat, and began counting their take. When he finished, he said, "Not as much as I hoped for. Fifty-seven even." He fell silent for a moment as he figured the shares. "That's a little over eighty-five hundred for Palmetto, and about twenty-four thousand apiece for you and me."

"That's my day care center," said Keene. "I'm satisfied, man. You?"

"Yeah," said Moss. "Yeah, I'm cool." Suddenly he frowned. "What's that up ahead?"

A white man in overalls was in the middle of the narrow blacktop road, frantically flagging them down. Next to the road, an old pickup truck was overturned in a culvert.

"Go around him," Moss said.

"Maybe somebody's hurt, Moss."

"*We'll* be hurt if we don't get over the St. Gabriel bridge by nine o'clock. Go around him."

Keene Summers flicked his eyes from the frantic man to the overturned truck. Then he saw a child lying alongside the culvert. "Somebody's hurt, Moss. It's a kid. I'm stopping."

"Are you crazy!" Moss snapped, but it was too late: Keene was already grinding the car to a halt at the edge of the culvert.

"Can y'all help me?" the man pleaded as he ran up to them. "My little girl's hurt and my little boy's stuck inside the truck!"

"What happened?" asked Keene, leaping out. Cursing under his breath, Moss jumped out with him.

"Blew a tire," said the farmer.

"See about the girl, Moss," Keene said. "I'll try to get the boy out."

"I smell gasoline," Moss warned.

"Yeah, so do I—"

Keene slipped into the culvert next to the overturned truck. Through the windshield he saw a young boy lying wedged up against one door. The door was locked but the window was down several inches. "Come help me!" Keene shouted to the farmer. Keene had begun to sweat with fear; the frightening odor of gasoline was almost overpowering.

The farmer slid down beside him. With four hands exerting pressure, they managed to force the window down far enough for Keene to reach in and unlock the door. They got the unconscious boy out and scrambled back up the embankment.

"How's the girl?" Keene asked.

"I think she's got a broken arm," Moss said, kneeling, helping the tearful child sit up.

Keene turned to the farmer. "Where's the nearest hospital?"

"Over by the St. Gabriel bridge."

"Which side?" Moss asked with sudden interest.

"This side," said the farmer.

"Come on, Moss," Keene said firmly. "These kids need attention."

They put the farmer and his little boy in the back seat. Moss cradled the little girl on his lap, and Keene drove. It was twenty miles to the outskirts of St. Gabriel, where the hospital was located. And the bridge. As they drove up to the hospital emergency entrance, Moss could see that there was as yet no roadblock on the bridge. "Let's make this fast," he said urgently to Keene. The black man threw him an irritated glance which he ignored.

Keene took the boy from his father and hurried into the emergency room, while Moss carried the sobbing girl right behind him. The trembling father of the children shouted for a doctor. It took a couple of minutes for nurses and attendants to get each of the children into an examining room. Moss saw a clock as he was being shown where to take the girl. It was ten before nine. Still got an edge, he thought tightly.

When the two children were finally in medical hands,

Moss took Keene firmly by the arm. "That's it, man. That's all we can do. Now let's split." They hurried back to where they had left the car. But as soon as they got outside the door, they saw that they were too late. A roadblock of two radio cars had sealed off the approach to the bridge. And a tall, uniformed policeman was walking around their car, looking it over. When they got close enough to him, they saw that his badge was inscribed: SHERIFF—ST. GABRIEL TOWNSHIP.

"This your car?" he asked, one hand on his pistol butt, his eyes shifting back and forth between them.

"Yes, sir, it is," Keene said, trying to keep the guilt out of his voice.

Moss said nothing. He felt ill, physically sick to his stomach. Dread thoughts of Angola flooded his head: the backbreaking field work, the lumpy mattresses, the smells and noise of hundreds of men, the long nights. He suddenly knew that he would rather die than go back to prison.

"What's that there drill on the back seat for?" the sheriff asked.

"We're steel workers," Keene replied. "Going down to New Orleans looking for work."

The sheriff's expression was inscrutable. "What's in the canvas bag on the front floorboard?" he asked.

Keene shrugged. "Just clothes, sir. Personal stuff."

"Suppose you open it and show me."

Moss hung his head and his shoulders slumped. Coley's words screamed inside his head: *You'll be old and gray before they let you out again.* He looked over at the sheriff's hand still on the pistol butt. *If I run, he'll put one right in my back,* Moss thought.

"Open the bag," the sheriff said again. Keene sighed resignedly and reached in the car for the bag. Just then, the father of the two injured children came out.

"My kids are gonna be all right," he said happily to Keene and Moss. Then he saw the sheriff. "Hey, Jesse," he greeted him.

"What are you doing here, Alvin?" the sheriff asked.

Alvin told him about the blowout, the rescue of the boy, driving both children to the hospital, carrying them inside. "Weren't for these two fellers, we might have lost Joesy. He's got a punctured lung and a concussion. Doc says he could've died of shock we didn't get him here quick as we did." He turned to Keene and Moss. "Fellers, this here's my brother Jesse. He's the sheriff hereabouts. I swear, I don't know how in the world to thank you boys for what you done."

"That's okay," Moss said, suddenly feeling all right again. "Your brother the sheriff knows how. Don't you, Sheriff?"

The sheriff nodded knowingly at Moss. "I reckon I do, all right."

"We was just telling him how we're in a hurry to be on our way to New Orleans to look for work. Weren't we, Sheriff?"

"That's a fact," the sheriff said. He moved his hand away from his gun. "Get in your car, boys. I'll ride with you and see you past the roadblock. Alvin, I'll be back directly to see the kids."

Half an hour later, Keene and Moss were well on their way home. Neither of them was making much conversation; it was taking them a while to get over the fright and nausea of almost being caught. But as they were driving past the New Orleans city limit, Moss felt the need to purge his conscience.

"You know that day I took the shank in my arm?" he said quietly. "I wasn't trying to keep that dude from sticking you. I thought he was coming for *me*. I had him confused with another one of those heavy dudes that I had a run-in with over some smokes that was owed me. Truth is, I hustled you into this job, Keene. You never really owed me nothing."

Keene swallowed dryly and did not say anything. He kept his anger in check, thinking: forgive and forget, it's all done with. He had the money to start the day care center now. The Lord moves in mysterious ways.

When they reached the Dixie Ezekiel Church, Moss carried the canvas bag in and opened it on Keene's desk. He counted out eighty-five hundred dollars.

"This is Palmetto's share; it goes to his lawyer. I want you to divide the rest in half. Your half you can start your day care center with or whatever you want to do. My half I want you to use to fix up that playground out there. I want it to look brand new again. And I want all new equipment bought; you can't play games without equipment, you know." Moss went to the door to leave. "If you want me for anything, I'll be working over at Coley's. As a fry cook."

Keene Summers was staring at his friend in disbelief. Moss paused at the door and bobbed his chin at the bag of money.

"This makes us even. It squares me for hustling you into the job, right?"

Keene smiled. "Right."

Moss winked and left the church. Outside, he ran into the little black boy with the shoeshine box.

"Hey, kid, good news," Moss told him. "The preacher is gonna fix up the playground. He's ordering all new equipment, too,"

The boy eyed Moss suspiciously. "You jiving me?"

"Hey, would I lie? Honest man like me?" Moss rubbed the boy's head and hurried off down the street.

On his way to the cafe, he began whistling "Just a Closer Walk With Thee," all the time wondering how long it would be until Jaysie turned eighteen.

It's not only the hardheads, ex-cons, smalltime fighters, and others on the underbelly of society who have to make the tough decisions in life that can affect them so markedly; sometimes it's the everyday, average, honest working man who gets caught up in one of life's webs and can't seem, no matter how great his effort and desire, to work his way out of it.

Such a man is Frank Holcomb, in a story that takes place in the western United States of the late 1950s, when five hundred dollars was a lot of money, and a respectable man, if desperate enough, might do something terribly repulsive for it....

The Marksman

Frank Holcomb was sitting by the stove in the kitchen of his ranch house, warming his hands around a cup of steaming coffee, staring out through the frost patterns on the windowpane as he waited for the phone to ring. It was not yet seven o'clock. The call, he knew, would come around seven; it always had.

Beyond the window he saw an early morning snow mist hover low over the flat pasture that stretched from his house to the mountains a mile away. It was pure white, billowy and rolling, like a thick, warm cloud, but Holcomb knew there was nothing thick or warm about it. The snow mist was thin and cold; walking through it would be like wading in ice water. Utah, he reflected, must be the coldest place in the world in January.

He put down his cup and lighted a cigarette. Exhaling the first deep drag, he turned to stare at the phone on the wall across the room. He did not know why he was so edgy waiting for it to ring. This time would be no different from the other—how many?—eight, yes—the other eight times. He sighed heavily, deciding that he was nervous simply because it had been so long. They had never gone two full years before this.

Upstairs he could hear Lill getting their daughter Bonnie up for school. Usually Lill had a difficult time of it with the girl on Monday mornings, but probably she would not on this particular Monday. This was the first day of school after the Christmas holiday; Bonnie was eager to show her classmates the new wristwatch she had found under the tree Christmas morning. She was certain, *absolutely* certain, that she would be the only girl to have a genuine self-winding heart-shaped young lady's wristwatch in the entire fourth grade.

The fourth grade, Holcomb pondered soberly; Bonnie was ten years old. That made him thirty-six. Lord, time passed quickly. He looked at the kitchen clock and saw that it still was not quite seven. *Years* passed quickly, he corrected himself; minutes seemed to drag by.

He heard Lill coming down the stairs; a moment later she entered the kitchen, chenille robe buttoned to the throat over her flannel pajamas.

"They haven't called yet?" she asked.

"No." He did not know why she asked, really; she would have heard the phone ring just as well upstairs as he would have in the kitchen.

"Maybe they won't," Lill said in a neutral tone, neither hopeful nor pessimistic.

Holcomb looked intently at his wife. She's a cool one, he thought admiringly. Always has been, come to think of it. Even the first time when he had told her what he was going to do, she had accepted it as if it were a thing *every* husband did; no surprise at all, no consternation, no arguments—just calm acceptance. Of course, that had been the year of the Big

The Marksman

Freeze, the year that winter had become a white death and left their cattle frozen stiff standing straight up, the year of no meat, no grain and no money. Maybe Lill had been as scared as he had been; maybe that was why she had not objected. That first time, with that first five hundred dollars he had earned, had carried them into spring and helped them save their ranch.

Then the second five hundred had paid for the doctor and the hospital when Bonnie came.

The third five hundred had bought the fence they needed to keep strays out of the west pasture, where the winter grass had to be protected.

The fourth five hundred had—

"I said," Lill repeated, "maybe they won't call."

"They'll call," Holcomb said. "Once it gets this close, they never back down. It's not like in some other places."

"If you go, what will you tell Bonnie?"

"Same thing I've always told her, I guess."

"She might be getting a little old for that story, mightn't she?"

"What do you mean?" Holcomb said, mildly indignant. "She's only ten. Besides, she always believes what her daddy tells her, you know that."

"All the same," Lill said, "I think you'd better give some thought to a new story. One of these days she's going to be old enough to put two and two together."

"Well," said Holcomb, "maybe by that time we'll be far enough ahead so I can quit—"

The phone rang.

Holcomb lifted the receiver before it could ring a second time. "Hello. Yes, operator, this is Frank Holcomb—"

A crisp businesslike voice came over the line. As he listened to the same words he had heard the other eight times,

Holcomb watched his wife. Her easy movements, the way she used her hands, the twist of her shoulders as she turned to do something, all were pleasing to Holcomb. For years he had secretly enjoyed watching her do the casual things that a woman does around her own house; the straightening, the arranging, the setting of a table as she was doing now. It gave Holcomb a warm feeling to see her moving about like that; it made him feel as if he *had* something.

"Yes, all right," he said into the phone when the crisp voice had finished. "I'll be there. Yes. Goodbye." He hung up and stood for a moment next to the phone.

"You're going?"

"Yes," he said, "I'm going." He stepped over to his place at the table and sat down. The smell of frying bacon filled the room. He heard his daughter coming down the stairs, and turned in his chair as she entered the kitchen. She walked directly to Holcomb and put her arms around his neck and kissed him on the cheek.

"Good morning, sweetheart," he said. hugging her back. He saw that she was wearing a Sunday dress instead of her usual woolen skirt and sweater. "Will she be warm enough in that?" he asked Lill.

"She can wear ski pants under it and take them off at school," his wife said. "It's the first day back and she's got her new watch on, you know."

Lill put a large platter of bacon and eggs and biscuits in the center of the table and they began eating breakfast.

"I can't wait to see how everyone likes my watch," Bonnie said excitedly. "It's such a pretty watch."

"Pretty watch for a pretty girl," said Holcomb. It wasn't true, really; she wasn't a very pretty girl. She was rather plain and had none of the full feminine features that made her mother so attractive. But she had the *lines*, Holcomb thought.

The Marksman

Her nose and mouth and eyes all had the right lines, and someday, seven or eight years from now, she would bloom into a very clean, very pretty young woman. Before then, he told himself silently, I will have to quit this business I'm involved in. It's one thing for her mother to know, but never—*never*—would he ever want Bonnie to find out.

"Daddy won't be home tonight," he said as casually as he could. "I have to go out of town and I won't be able to get back until sometime tomorrow afternoon."

"Where are you going?" the girl wanted to know. "Won't you be home to hear how everyone liked my watch?"

"You can tell me all about it tomorrow night. I have to take a trip up north. Fellow I know wants me to shoot a bad cat for him."

"A mountain lion?" Bonnie's voice grew breathless. Having grown up on a small cattle spread, she knew, even at ten, the hazards of a mountain cat.

"Not sure just what kind it is," said Holcomb. "Just know that it's a bad one."

"Aren't you glad you're such a good shot, daddy," the girl said, a little worshipful.

Holcomb did not answer.

They finished the meal and Lill started cleaning away the dishes. "You run along and get into your ski pants," she told Bonnie. "The school bus will be here in five minutes."

Holcomb remained at the table and sipped more coffee until Bonnie was bundled up for the trip to school and they heard the familiar honk of the school bus as it came slowly down the snow-covered road. Holcomb and his wife kissed their daughter at the door and watched through the window as she ran awkwardly along the slippery path to the road, waved briefly, them disappeared inside the bright orange vehicle. It moved off sluggishly before a trail of billowing exhaust and a moment later was gone.

"Well," Holcomb said, almost to himself, "better get ready, I guess."

"I'll get your bag and other things from upstairs," Lill said.

"All right."

As Lill went up the stairs, Holcomb walked into a spare room they called their den and unlocked his gun cabinet. There were five weapons in the rack: two shotguns and three rifles. Holcomb removed one of the rifles and laid it on a table next to a jigsaw puzzle he and Lill and Bonnie had been working on since Christmas. The puzzle, nearly complete, was a picture of a beautiful ballerina standing tall and graceful with arms upstretched in the classic ballet pose. The gleaming, deadly rifle looked frighteningly incongruous lying next to the sedate picture, but Holcomb did not notice. He sat down and with a small screwdriver prepared to disassemble the weapon.

The rifle Holcomb worked on had a smooth, solid walnut stock mounted under a cold forged barrel twenty-three inches long. The receiver and bolt and trigger housing all were chrome plated, as were the swivels that held tautly the pliable black leather sling at the gun's belly. There was a matted ramp sight at the front of the muzzle, and a dual range peep sight at the rear of the breech. A spring magazine, blued, lay snugly in its niche beneath the chamber entry. At that moment the magazine was empty; later on it would hold five 30-30 caliber, 220-grain, steel jacketed, semi-pointed bullets.

Lill came in with Holcomb's overnight bag just as he finished breaking down the rifle and was placing the parts neatly into a fleece-lined takedown case.

"I put in a clean shirt and socks for you to wear on the train coming back," she said. "Also extra handkerchiefs, your bat-

The Marksman

tery shaver, and four packs of cigarettes."

"*Four* packs?"

"You ran out and had to look for a place to buy some last time, remember?"

"That's right, I forgot." She's a cool one, all right, Holcomb thought again. But it pleased him that she took care to remember so many things regarding his comfort. Every man should have a woman like her. He zipped up the gun case and laid it in the open suitcase Lill had brought in.

"Guess that's about it."

Lill followed him into the front hall where he opened the closet to get out his heavy mackinaw.

"Will it be colder up there than down here?"

"Most likely. Usually is."

Holcomb slipped a pair of fur earmuffs over his head before putting on his hat. He wrapped a wool muffler around his neck, turned up the collar of his coat and drew on a pair of deerskin gloves lined with rabbit fur.

"Keep the doors locked and leave a light on all night," he said, the same thing he had said the other eight times he had gone away. "I'll be back around three tomorrow if the trains run on time."

Holcomb gave his wife a warm, soft, lingering kiss. He left the house then and trudged off across the frozen snow, suitcase in hand, toward the barn to get out the pickup for the drive to town to the depot.

Spaak met him when he got off the train.

"Hello, Holcomb."

"Hello, Spaak."

It was night now. Holcomb had been on the train for eleven hours. The northern air was bitterly cold.

"Car's over this way," Spaak said. Holcomb walked with

him along the wooden passenger platform and down three railroad-tie steps to where a car waited with its motor idling. "Always leave it running," Spaak explained, "so's the heater'll stay warm."

Holcomb nodded. He had heard the same thing before from Spaak. Eight times before, to be exact. Opening the car door on the right side, he laid his bag on the back seat and got in. Spaak swung the car in a slow arc away from the depot and eased it up a cinder-covered drive to the highway.

"What's the temperature?" Holcomb wanted to know.

" 'Bout six, I reckon," Spaak said clinically, "maybe five. When it gets under ten it don't make much difference anyway."

"Guess you're right," Holcomb agreed. He settled back in the seat, loosening his collar and muffler and taking off the earmuffs, and lighted a cigarette.

The road they drove was a two-lane blacktop, piled high on each side with a continuous mound of snow laid out almost geometrically perfect by the blade of a snowplow. It was a straight level road, and although Holcomb had never traveled it except at night, he knew it cut across the flat plane of a high valley, through pastures and meadows and grazing land much like that of his own place far to the south. The land was vast, and sweeping, stretching to lofty, white-topped mountains on all sides, the high altitude air thin and pure and, like the land, rich. Maybe, Holcomb thought, when it was all over, when he had quit and been away from it for a few years, he would bring Lill and Bonnie up here for a vacation, just to see what it did look like in the daytime.

"You follow pro football much?" Spaak asked in an attempt to make conversation.

"Not much," Holcomb told him. They had been all through this before, he recalled, trying to make conversation and failing miserably at it because, although they had known each other for longer than eleven years, they were absolute strangers. Apart from their brief association at times like this, they never saw one another and thus had never established any common ground between them. It was a shame too, Holcomb thought, because Spaak seemed likable enough, and undoubtedly there could be found many things of mutual interest, such as hunting, which was common to nearly all men in Utah. Because of Holcomb's unique position in their association, however, he was precluded from discussing anything like that, anything in the least way personal that might give an indication of who he was, where he lived, whether he had a family, a business.

To Spaak, Holcomb had to remain simply Holcomb, that was all: a name, and a man who answered to it. Spaak did not even know exactly how Holcomb was summoned; all he knew was that on the night he was needed, Holcomb would arrive. He would arrive on a train that had sped the length of the state; he might have come from anywhere. To Spaak, the man called Holcomb was really little more than a specter.

"How 'bout a little music?" Spaak said reaching for the radio.

"Fine," said Holcomb. They were about halfway there now, he guessed. It wouldn't be much longer. He rested his head back against the seat and closed his eyes. The radio warmed up and soft music filtered out of the speaker. Between the soothing melody of the music and the lulling sound of the car cutting the wind, Holcomb soon dozed.

He awoke when he felt the car slowing to a halt. Opening his eyes he saw in the glare of the headlights the gate being opened for them.

"We're there," Spaak said quietly, seeing that Holcomb was awake.

"All right." Holcomb sat up and reached inside his coat for a cigarette.

They passed through the gate and across a snow-covered courtyard to a small very narrow wooden shack; three wooden walls built onto a wooden floor and supporting a flat wooden roof. Where the fourth wall should have been was a partition four feet high; the opening between it and the roof was covered with a length of burlap.

Spaak parked the car directly beside the shack and put it in neutral, pulling on the parking brake and leaving the motor running. Holcomb adjusted his muffler and buttoned his mackinaw; he did not bother with the earmuffs this time. Turning in the seat, he flipped open his bag and removed the rifle case. Spaak got out of the car and came around to open the door on Holcomb's side. Cradling the rifle case in the crook of one arm, Holcomb stepped out into the thin, bitter cold of the high Utah night.

Spaak pulled open a narrow door and Holcomb followed him into the shack. Inside was an atmosphere of dull, greenish light, emanating from a large oil lantern suspended on the wall. Aside from the lantern, the shack was completely empty, totally bare.

"I'll tell 'em you're here," Spaak said. Holcomb nodded and Spaak left the shack.

When he was alone, Holcomb stood for a moment in the quiet emptiness, smelling the cold pungence of the freshly sawed lumber of which the shack was built. He breathed deeply of the smell, because it was pleasant to his senses, like the smell of fresh hay and of the high woods country where he hunted. He wondered briefly how it would feel to know that the new wood of the shack would be the last thing he would ever smell; to know that he was going to die with that rich, vigorous scent in his nostrils, a final reminder of just how precious life was.

There was a sudden flapping sound and Holcomb turned to the half wall that had the length of burlap stretched across its opening. A corner of the burlap had come loose from its nail and was being whipped back by a shaft of wind from the open courtyard outside. Stepping over to the partition, Holcomb forced the truant corner back tightly over the head of the nail. He did not try to look beyond the burlap; what was there he would see soon enough.

With a sigh, Holcomb turned and knelt beside the back wall, placing his rifle case on the floor and unzipping it. Removing his gloves, he spread open the wings of the case and began to assemble the rifle.

When Spaak returned a few minutes later, Holcomb was leaning against the wall smoking a cigarette. The fully assembled rifle rested, muzzle down, between his hip and one arm.

" 'Bout ready," Spaak said.

Holcomb nodded. He took a final deep drag on the cigarette, brushed the ash off with his thumb and put the butt in his pocket. He could as easily have dropped it on the floor, but he had a fetish about these shacks, this one and the other eight in which he had stood; he did not like to leave anything of himself behind.

The shack door opened and a small man wearing a hat and heavy overcoat entered.

"Holcomb," he said, bobbing his head in brusque acknowledgment. He drew one hand out of his overcoat pocket and handed Holcomb five brass-colored, steel-tipped, 30-30 cartridges. While both he and Spaak watched, Holcomb slid them into a spring magazine and inserted it into the belly of the rifle. He loosened the sling, slipped his left arm into it, and tightened it across his muscle.

"Ready?"

Holcomb wet his lips and nodded. He turned and faced the partition as Spaak turned off the lantern and began removing the burlap. This was the worst part of it for Holcomb; not the actual squeezing of the trigger, but the two to three minutes between the time he was ready and—

The shack door closed behind him and he knew that he and Spaak were alone again. The burlap was all the way off now; an icy draft flooded the narrow room. In a moment, Holcomb thought, the floods will go on. He tried to close his eyes but could not. Always it was the same; he *wanted* to close his eyes, but his eyelids would never function.

This is the last time, he swore to himself. *The last time—*

The area beyond the partition was flooded with sudden light—stark, glaring light from powerful floodlights. Before Holcomb's wide eyes a scene of horror was illuminated. A second three-sided enclosure, lumber-new like the first, stood a scant twenty feet away, its open side facing the floodlights and the half-wall behind which Holcomb waited. Within the structure a crude, heavy wooden chair had been built of the same raw timber, a chair of flat, hard planes, without contours, without dignity. A man was strapped to the chair, his forearms, thighs, calves and chest bound to the new wood with leather belts. A black hood covered his head and fell to his waist. Pinned to the dark cloth, over the man's heart, was a four-inch target.

Last time, Holcomb vowed again. *I won't do it anymore.*

He tore his eyes away from the hooded figure in the chair and nervously scanned the rest of the cold midnight scene. A dozen men, witnesses, stood still as statues to one side of the execution shack, their faces turned away from Holcomb, the wind whipping at their coattails and swirling gusts of powdery snow around their feet. Four guards armed with shotguns stood between the witnesses and the shack. A doctor, stethoscope in hand, huddled near the guards. A Mormon bishop, hatless, moved his lips silently.

Holcomb lowered his eyes and stared at the partition in front of him. He thought of home, of Lill, of Bonnie; Bonnie, growing up so quickly, so few years left for her to be daddy's little girl. Suppose she found out someday . . .

Outside the shack, the man who had given Holcomb the bullets stepped into the side light of one of the floodlights. He put on a pair of glasses and held up a document from which he began to read aloud.

"Order of Execution. The Supreme Court of the Sovereign State of Utah, having found . . ."

The wind whistled into the shack where Holcomb stood. The sound of it muted some of the hurried, official words, but it did not matter to Holcomb; he had heard them all eight times before.

". . . murder in the first degree, and having been duly sentenced in the Superior Court of the County of . . ."

The words droned on and the wind whipped and whistled while the guards stood erect, the doctor waited patiently, the bishop continued to move his lips, and the witnesses shuffled uneasily as death drew near.

Then it was silent, starkly silent; even the wind stopped. The little corner of the prison courtyard became for the men the stillest place in the world.

"Ready . . ."

Holcomb raised the rifle and dug its butt into his shoulder. A trickle of sweat escaped from his armpit and ran slowly, distractingly down his side.

". . . aim . . ."

From beneath the black hood of the man in the chair, a sob escaped. It pierced the thin night air like the slash of a blade.

". . . fire!"

Holcomb squeezed off the first round and saw a hole appear dead center in the target; the body behind the target lurched violently. Holcomb's hand worked the bolt fluidly, ejecting the spent shell, throwing another one into the chamber.

Last time . . .

He flexed his sensitive trigger finger and fired again. And again and again and again.

In the car, with Spaak driving him back to the depot where he would have a three-hour wait for the morning train, Holcomb's thoughts settled again on his little ranch and his little family. If he had a good year this year—that is if he did better than break even after all the expenses, if he could manage to put a few hundred in the bank—then at the end of the year he would write a letter to the prison bureau and tell them to find someone else for the job. He would quit; quit for good, and get out of it once and for all.

Settling more comfortably in the seat, Holcomb reached into his shirt pocket for a cigarette. His fingers brushed against the voucher for five hundred dollars that the warden had given him. If he mailed the voucher to the state paymaster that afternoon when he got home, he'd have his check in about a week. He had hoped to be able to use the money for a good stock bull to build up his herd, but thinking of it now, he did not see how he would be able to. The electric pump on his well was going bad and would surely need replacing by spring; a hailstorm had damaged the roof of the barn last month and he had to buy material to repair that; and Lill had mentioned a couple of times that maybe they should see about braces for Bonnie because a couple of her front teeth were turning crooked. So most of the five hundred would go for those things and probably a few others he hadn't even thought of.

He could not help thinking, though, how nice it would have been to buy that bull. Just a little more good blood in his stock and he soon would have a prime line of beef. Then he wouldn't have to sell through stock jobbers anymore and give away twenty percent of his profit; he could take a trip to the Chicago stockyards and get himself lined up with one of the top grade beef buyers and be able to sell directly for premium market price. Of course a trip to Chicago would take money too. Everything took money . . .

Holcomb rubbed his chin thoughtfully and turned to Spaak.

"How many more you got up there in the death house now?" he asked casually.

"Three," said Spaak. "Probably be four pretty soon. Fellow over in Provo was convicted last week of killing an Indian woman; ain't been sentenced yet, but he'll probably get the max. Federal government's touchy about their Indians getting murdered, and the state court knows it. Yeah, he'll get the max for sure."

"But right now you've got three?"

"Yep. Right now three."

That was fifteen hundred dollars worth, Holcomb thought. A man could do a lot on a little ranch with fifteen hundred dollars.

Another story of camaraderie among returned combat veterans such as the ones in **OLD SOLDIERS**, *but this time it concerns four ex-Marines in the days following service in Vietnam, where chemical canisters marked with an orange stripe had been used to defoliate the jungle before troops moved in.*

Four men who have gone back to their respective lives, but who find that the grueling, obscene war they left behind is still with them: in their minds, their spirits, their personalities, and especially their bodies—and that it may even still be killing some of them . . .

The Color of Death

When the phone rang at four o'clock in the morning, Joe Page knew instinctively that it was Billy calling. He could not have explained *how* he knew—he just knew. The first several rings of the phone started bringing Joe's mind up from the Quaalude nest in which it rested; the next several rings generated movement in limbs that were wasted from an earlier sexual marathon with a woman with fuchsia hair lying next to him; and somewhere around the eighth or tenth ring he sat up on the side of the open sleeper sofa and picked up the receiver.

"Yeah, hello—"

"Joe? Is that you, Joe? This here's Billy."

"Yeah, Billy—"

"Listen, Joe, you 'member those lumps I had on my legs last year? Those ones that the doctor said was just fatty tumors that would prob'ly go away—"

"The ones that did go away," Joe reminded him.

"Yeah, well, they're back," Billy said. A Tennessee twang

made his voice go high-pitched sometimes, like when he was agitated. "When I woke up this morning, I had 'em on both legs again. And I can feel some starting on my back."

Joe did not say anything. He was trying to visualize Billy, trying to picture him on the Tennessee sharecropper farm, wearing overalls, sitting on a tractor in the sun. But the only image that came to mind was the other Billy; the Billy with a gun in his hand; the Billy who killed men.

"Joe? Did you hear me? I said—"

"I heard you, Billy. You'd better go back to the hospital."

"I don't like the hospital, Joe. They act like I'm some kind of nuisance or something. Anyhow, they don't help me none."

"You have to go back," Joe said patiently. He massaged the back of his neck. The woman next to him stirred and expelled a heavy breath.

"Joe, I think Chief Charlie is dead," Billy said, changing the subject. "I ain't had a letter from him in two months. Only reason he'd quit writing me was if he died."

"Maybe he's on a drunk," Joe suggested. "Maybe he's in jail. You know how Indians are."

"He's dead, Joe. I can feel it."

"Okay, have it your way. Now what about the hospital? When can you go back?"

"Will you come and go with me, Joe?" Billy asked. "That time you went with me, they didn't treat me so bad."

"I can't, Billy. It's too far. Besides, I've got a new job."

"A new job? No bull? What kind of job?"

Joe thought fast. "I'm managing a string of parking lots. Couple of dozen lots. All over the L. A. area."

"No bull?" Billy's voice became excited. "Are any of 'em in Hollywood?"

"Yeah, two or three." The one at which he was a parking

attendant was in Culver City, the pits.

"You ever see Ann-Margret?"

"Saw her just the other day."

"She look as gorgeous in person?"

"Better."

"No bull! Man—!" Billy's voice trailed off. He was silent for several moments. Then he said, "I guess you couldn't get a few days off and go to the hospital with me then?"

"I don't think so. But I want you to promise me you'll go anyway."

"Oh, sure."

"Word of honor?"

"Sure, Joe. Listen, I gotta get out in the patch and tend my crop. I'll talk to you soon."

Billy hung up and Joe sat in the dark holding the receiver, thinking about the lumps on Billy's legs and back. He wondered why people at the hospital didn't treat him any better. Goddamned doctors and nurses; coldest people in the world.

Hanging up the phone, Joe rose and moved a few feet across the room to a tiny alcove kitchen set behind a breakfast bar. Turning on a light over the sink, he ran cold water and washed his face, then drank some of it from cupped hands to irrigate the desert inside his mouth caused by the Quaalude. Why were those lumps coming back on Billy's legs, he wondered. And why had Chief Charlie stopped writing to Billy? Could Billy be right; was the Chief dead?

A slant of light from the kitchen alcove fell across the woman on the sleeper sofa. Joe saw that she had dragged the sheet partly off to expose one flaccid breast. She was breathing nosily now through her open mouth, and there were bubbles of spittle collecting in one corner of her lips. During their earlier sexual ten-rounder, her breasts—*her?* What the hell was her name anyway? Her breasts had been tight with a high threshold of pain, her lips punk purple and forming a perpetual circle of desire. She had parked her Corvette on his lot that afternoon, they had talked, and she had picked him up at nine when he closed. Between the fuchsia hair, purple lips, those breasts, and the 'ludes, he had made it though another night. Another night that would become meaningless in a week, forgotten in a month. Or perhaps it was already meaningless; if a man could not even remember a woman's name—

Billy was scared, Joe realized, interrupting his own train of thought. Joe recognized the fear in the Tennessean's voice; he had heard it before. Like everybody else, Billy feared the things he could not understand: the lumps that had returned on his body; the cessation of letters from Chief Charlie.

He won't go back to the hospital, Joe decided. Billy's sour Southern pride would not let him go back to a place where he thought he was considered a nuisance. Unless somebody went with him for support.

Joe walked back to the telephone and held the handset toward the light to dial, wondering if Billy had left the house yet. But Billy answered on the first ring and Joe thought: He was sitting there waiting for me to call.

"Listen, I can probably take a few days off—"

"You gonna be driving back?" Billy asked.

"Yeah—"

"Could you stop off and see what's the matter with the Chief? It won't be out of your way."

"Okay." Joe shook his head resignedly. Billy had taken it for granted that he would call; taken it for granted that he would find out for him about Chief Charlie. In Billy's mind, Joe was still the leader. A follower had a right to take his leader for granted.

After he hung up the second time, Joe looked at the clock

and calculated that there were a couple of hours before the morning rush began. Might as well get out of town ahead of the traffic, he decided. Ever since he got back from Vietnam, he realized, he had been getting out of town ahead of *something:* creditors, irate husbands, bench warrants. Lately he had developed the habit of never looking back, in case somebody was gaining on him.

Quietly, so as not to wake the woman with fuchsia hair, Joe Page began packing.

Heat rose from the Arizona highway in shimmering waves, and just outside Casa Grande a rattlesnake slithered across the asphalt in front of Joe's car. Joe slowed down to let it get across his side, but in the rearview mirror saw a pickup truck swerve into the oncoming lane to run over it. Bastard, Joe thought. For the next few miles he entertained violent thoughts about the driver of the pickup.

A gravel road led from the state highway out to the Pima reservation. The reservation settlement was an accumulation of faded surplus government structures; mostly pre-fab Quonset huts with rusted corrugated roofs and porches that had tilted with the shifting of the desert. The only sign of life was a trio of Pima men in old jeans and tee shirts, sitting in the shade of a two-pump gas station playing cards on an upturned Valvoline carton. A thermometer nearby, also in the shade, registered one hundred-eight. Joe recalled Chief Charlie telling him that this was a place, the older Pimas believed, that long ago became so hot that the trees melted and formed cactus.

Parking, Joe let the dust settle before getting out of the car, then went up three wooden steps to a Quonset with a sign on the outside that read: TRIBAL OFFICES. At a badly scarred desk inside sat a Pima man of perhaps forty wearing a plaid shirt and a belt with a large silver buckle. He had a pot-belly and thick hips from too much sitting. On the desk in front of him was an open Dr. Pepper and a skin magazine; behind him on a table was a small black-and-white television turned to a game show he was not watching.

"What you need?" he asked when Joe entered.

"I'm looking for Charles Long," Joe said. "I think he lives somewhere on the reservation."

"What you want him for?"

The curtness of the question rankled Joe but he did not show it. "I'm a friend of his. I was driving through and thought—"

"Charlie Long's dead, man." The Indian said it without emotion, like he would say your battery was dead. "His old man and sister live a few miles down the road, if you want to see them. It's a house on the left with an old Studebaker up on blocks out in front. You can't miss it." As Joe turned to leave, the man was suddenly inspired to ask, "Say, you don't happen to know if he had insurance of any kind, do you? Half of it's supposed to go to the tribal council if he had any. His old man said there wasn't none, but he could be lying."

"I wouldn't know about any insurance," Joe replied evenly, and left.

Outside, Joe quickly decided not to visit Chief Charlie's father and sister. No point to it, he thought. He had found out what he came to find out: the Chief was dead, just as Billy suspected. The important thing now was to get to Tennessee and take Billy back to the hospital.

In the car, Joe checked his roadmap and found that he could continue through the reservation and connect with the Interstate on the other side, without doubling back. Driving away from the tribal office, he tried to visualize Charlie here on the Pima reservation, wearing old jeans and a tee shirt, playing cards in the shade at the two-pump gas station. But the only image that came to mind was the other Charlie; the Charlie with the gun in his hand; the Charlie who killed men. Why, he wondered, could he never think of Billy or Charlie as the way they had *become,* instead of the way they had *been.* Odell Sampson, a black man from Chicago, who had been the fourth member of their team, had once told them it would not matter that they stopped killing—they would still be killers. "Once you lose that cherry, baby, you never a virgin again," Odell had said. "A killer *always* be a killer." Maybe, Joe mused, Odell had been right. Whenever Joe saw Billy or Chief Charlie or even Odell in his mind, it was always with a gun in their hands. Joe avoided thinking about himself.

A couple of miles farther along, Joe came to the reservation cemetery. On impulse he pulled off the road and parked. Without knowing why, he wanted to see Charlie's grave. Randomly he began prowling the parched lanes between rows of bleached headstones and grave markers. The brutal mid-afternoon sun at once became scorching on the scalp under his thinning hair, and on his nose where he always sunburned first. He had no hat of any kind; common sense told him he should get back out of the sun, but for some indefinable reason he kept going; he *had* to see the grave. Like a specter he continued to walk, his eyes flicking from dead name to dead name.

Suddenly his eyes stopped and held. Not on Charlie's grave but on another. A name from the past. The marker read: IRA HAMILTON HAYES. Joe stared at the name. Ira Hayes was the Pima Indian who had been one of five Marines who planted the United States flag atop Mt. Suribachi on Iwo Jima. The photograph of them doing it had become famous; the men and their act were forever preserved life-size in a bronze statue in Washington, D.C. Ira Hayes had returned to the barren land of his tribe a national figure, and died there an alcoholic unable to help his people secure irrigation for their parched land, unable to cope with his own hollow fame—hero to the Pima, red-skinned nigger to Arizona whites—and ultimately unable to help even himself as the liquor took more and more control. One night he had fallen to the ground drunk with his face in a puddle of rare rainwater and drowned in the middle of the desert. Chief Charlie had told the story to Joe and the others; they had all been quietly moved by it.

Joe walked on, up and down the rows, for another ten minutes. At one point he was surprised to find a young Pima girl, perhaps fourteen, sitting in the shade of one of the taller gravestones. She had waist-length hair black and shiny as a crow's wing, and eyes like perfect bullet holes. Her jeans were cut off at mid-thigh and the simple white blouse she wore was sleeveless. Her bare feet were dusty up to the ankle. She watched Joe but said nothing to him. Without speaking to her, he continued on his way. In the very next row, Joe found Charlie's grave. It had a simple square marker at its head giving his name, Charles Edward Long, the tribe, Casa Grande Pima, and dates of birth and death. Joe stood looking at the grave, aware that the young Pima girl was watching him. But for her presence, he would have said something to Charlie; nothing philosophical or sage; nothing heavy—just "So long, it's been good to know you," or something like that. But with the girl within hearing he was too self-conscious, so he simply thought his words, then turned to leave.

"Why did you stop at my brother's grave?" the Pima girl asked. Her words seemed very loud in the hot silence of the place. Joe stopped and turned to her.

"He was a friend." He studied her dark, angular features, seeing nothing of Charlie in her face. Her name, he remembered Charlie saying, was Luz.

"Are you Billy?" she asked eagerly.

"No. I'm Joe Page."

"Oh. You were the leader."

Joe nodded. "Yes."

The girl looked wistfully at Charlie's grave. "I thought maybe you were Billy. When Charles died, I wanted to write and tell Billy about it. But my father wouldn't let me. He said if Billy was a true friend to Charles, he would come here to see why Charles stopped writing."

"Billy's sick again," Joe explained. "He has to go back to the hospital."

"Oh." She rose and came over to him, her height surprising him; she was all legs and arms, elbows and knees. "Charles went to the hospital before he died, but they said they couldn't do anything for him."

"What was the matter with him?" Joe asked.

The girl shrugged. "Nobody knows. He had funny lumps all over his body."

Joe drove the rest of the way to Tennessee as if he was in an endurance race. Across New Mexico, the Texas panhandle, Oklahoma, and Arkansas; filling up with gas, buying vending machine food, and using the rest room all at one station, other than that only stopping when clawing sleep made further driving too dangerous, in which case he simply pulled off the road wherever he was and slept for an hour, two at the most. It was seven in the morning when he drove around the town square of Ripley, Tennessee, and asked at the Blue Star Cafe how to find the farm Billy worked. It was sixteen miles down in the bottom land along a tributary of the Mississippi. Rich cotton land. When Joe got there, he found a wide field of healthy stalks budding with bolls already splitting to expose their fluffy white treasure. A frame shack was set in the middle of the field and Billy, in bib overalls, sat in a rocker on the porch, waiting for him.

"Chief's dead, ain't he?" Billy asked without preliminary when Joe got out of the car.

Joe nodded without speaking and stepped up onto the porch. Billy rose and the two men embraced. They held each other as brothers might, their affection deep and genuine.

"How do you feel?" Joe asked when they separated.

"Not too hot," Billy admitted. He was a lanky man with a perpetual stoop. "I been having some—what do you call it?—when you feel sick?"

"Nausea."

"Yeah. I been having some nausea."

"Why don't you get ready," Joe suggested," and we'll leave for the hospital right away."

"Don't you want to get some rest? You look thrashed, man."

"I'm okay. Let's leave now."

Billy shrugged. "If you say so." Joe was still the leader.

Billy changed into a pair of khakis and a sport shirt, threw some extra things into a suitcase, and they started off. The hospital was a hundred and fifty miles away, a three-hour drive. Halfway there they pulled into a truck stop for breakfast. In a booth by the window they asked the waitress for two orders of sausage and scrambled eggs.

"Two number fours," she said and walked away.

Joe watched Billy shift around trying to get comfortable. "Do the lumps hurt?" he asked.

Billy shook his head. "They ain't got no feeling in 'em at all. Just feels funny to lean back on them. Gushy, like."

The waitress returned and set two glasses of orange juice on the table. Billy's expression darkened. "We didn't order that, miss."

"It comes with the number four."

"I don't care what it comes with. We don't want it."

"There's no extra charge—"

Billy glared at her. "You understand English? *We—don't—want—it!*"

The waitress's lips compressed. "Well, there's no need to get nasty about it. I mean, after *all*."

The fry cook came out of the kitchen. He had muscular arms and tattoos. "What's the problem, Thelma?"

"Some people just don't know the meaning of the word courtesy," Thelma said tightly.

"Go to hell, both of you," Billy told them. He got up and walked away from the booth. The fry cook scowled and looked like he might go after him, so Joe rose and blocked his way.

"He's sick, mister. He didn't mean anything by it. Here—" He gave the fry cook ten dollars for the breakfasts, and the waitress five for her hurt feelings.

Back in the car, Billy said, "I'm sorry, Joe. I just couldn't look at that juice. It's the color of death."

"I know," Joe said. "It's okay."

At the hospital, they put Billy through six hours of tests: x-rays, blood study, urinalysis, cardiogram, hearing and vision tests, even a sperm count—which Billy at first balked at, but finally consented to. They also did biopsies of minute plugs taken from the fatty lumps on his back and legs. When it was all over, the doctor told Billy the same thing he had told him three times before.

"The lumps are just fatty tissue. There's no carcinoma, no blood infection, no indication whatever that they're affecting any critical function of the body. And certainly nothing to lead us to believe that Agent Orange was in any way a causal factor."

The Color of Death

Billy looked down at his hands, folded in his lap. Joe, sitting next to him, asked, "What about the nausea? And the friend of ours who died in Arizona with lumps on his body too?"

"Nausea," the doctor said, "can be caused by dozens of conditions. Too much sugar, not enough sugar, too much salt, not enough salt," he waved a hand peremptorily, "even too much sex or not enough sex. As for your friend in Arizona, I couldn't comment on his death without first studying his medical record. But I know this: if his condition had been positively linked to Agent Orange, this hospital would have been advised—"

"Unless the government wanted to cover it up," Joe interjected.

The doctor fixed him in a cool stare. "Are you a relative of this patient?" he asked pointedly. "Or his attorney or what?"

"I'm the man," Joe replied evenly, "who led him and the others into the strip of jungle that had been defoliated. I was his fire team leader."

The doctor sighed quietly and put aside his irritation. "Look, men, I'm not trying to handle you or con you. If there was medical proof that Agent Orange was at fault, why, I'd be the first one to certify not only treatment but a disability pension as well. But there's simply nothing to back up such a claim. We wouldn't know how to treat you anyway, other than to surgically remove the lumps. Hell, we don't even know *what's* causing them; maybe it was the Marine Corps chow, or the Thai pot and hash and other stuff you guys smoked over there, or maybe the other side was engaging in some kind of chemical warfare that we don't know about. Some men," he pointed at Joe, "haven't been affected at all." He spread his hands helplessly. "Agent Orange was a mixture of two defoliants, one of which contained a chemical called dioxin. It has been tested extensively and shown to have numerous adverse effects on laboratory animals—lymphomas, gastritis, impotence, liver failure—but it has *never* been proven harmful to humans. The only medically proven condition definitely associated with human exposure to dixoin is chloracne, a skin rash. Human tissue simply does not retain the chemical long enough for it to do more serious damage."

Billy stared at the doctor for a moment, finally grunted softly as if he himself were stupid to have expected anything better, and walked out of the office. Rising to follow him, Joe paused long enough to say, "The bottom line for Billy is still no medical treatment, no disability, no nothing—is that it?"

"For the present time, I'm afraid so," the doctor confirmed. "At some time in the future—"

"He doesn't have a future," Joe interrupted. "Can't you see that? He's dying right now."

As Joe left, the doctor wanted to say how sorry he was. But he could not muster the words.

Outside in the car, Billy stared solemnly at the dashboard and said, "Somebody's to blame for this, Joe. Somebody ought to pay."

Now it was Joe who grunted softly. "Who?" he asked.

Billy shrugged. "I don't know. Somebody."

"There's nobody," Joe asserted. "The President that sent us over there is dead. I don't even remember who the Secretary of Defense was, or the Secretary of State, but they were just advisors anyway. And we can't go after all the politicians that let the war go on for so long. Or the Joint Chiefs of Staff. Or the Commandant of the Marine Corps. Or the admiral who ordered the stuff sprayed—"

"What about Lightman?" Billy asked.

"The colonel?"

"He's the one sent us into it," Billy reminded. "We could've gone around the strip that they sprayed. Lt. Russo asked permission to send us the long way around—"

"We didn't have enough time," Joe said. "We had to check out that village before the main force moved up, in case it was mined."

"Another day wouldn't have made no difference," Billy argued. "Lightman just wouldn't have looked as good to the top brass."

Joe frowned, remembering Colonel Ralph Lightman, the martinet Marine officer who had been in charge of their unit. "Lightning" Lightman, they called him. He wore pearl-handled pistols and carried a swagger stick with a Japanese bullet on its tip that had been pulled out of his shoulder on Saipan. The top brass always gave him the dirty jobs to do because they knew he could get his men to do them. Most Marines in his Force Recon group would have gone to hell for him. Maybe some even did, Joe mused. A living hell like Chief Charlie had gone through, like Billy was going through now.

"Another day wouldn't have made no difference," Billy repeated doggedly. " 'Cept to us." He stared starkly at Joe. "He ought to have to pay."

Joe's frown deepened and he said quietly, "I'm not sure, Billy. I'm just not sure."

"Let's make sure then." Billy took a roadmap out of the glove compartment and unfolded it. Studying it, he said, "Looks like about six hundred miles to Chicago." No further explanation was necessary.

Joe nodded. "Think you can drive?" he asked. Billy shook his head.

"I don't think so, Joe. I'm feeling worse all the time. Kind of dizzy-like, you know—"

"Lie down in the back seat; maybe you can sleep."

Billy got into the back seat. "Don't let me die by myself, Joe."

"I won't," Joe promised.

The trip north took fifteen hours, Joe again making only necessary multi-purpose stops for gas, food and men's room visits. It was nine o'clock in the morning when they drove slowly along a tenement block on Chicago's south side. Several unfriendly black faces paused on the sidewalk to look at them as they pulled to the curb and parked.

"We better hope he still lives here," Billy said apprehensively. He was now riding up front with Joe. The hostile dark faces generated an inbred Southern nervousness.

Joe glanced around. Half a dozen black men and women had come out onto nearby porches to stare at them. Windows had been raised and others leaned out to look. It was as if their color had reflected a signal of some kind that warned: Outsider. Intruder. White man.

On the front steps of the building Joe and Billy were looking for, three sullen young black men, all wearing red sweatbands, glared threateningly. As Joe and Billy got out of the car and started up the steps, one of them said, "Say man, you lost or what?"

"We're looking for someone," Joe said by way of reply. "A man named Odell Sampson." Joe waited a long moment for some kind of response, but none was forthcoming. He finally had to ask specifically, "Do you know Odell Sampson?"

Before the youth could answer, a nearby female voice said, "I know Odell Sampson." Joe and Billy turned to an open window on the first floor where they saw a woman of perhaps sixty with her head wrapped in a neatly tied blue bandanna. She had a strong, smoldering face and a defiantly raised chin.

"What y'all want with Odell Sampson?"

The two white men went up to the porch, close to the window. "We're friends of Odell's," Joe said.

The woman shook her head adamantly. "Odell ain't got no white friends."

"He used to have," Joe said. "In the Vietnam War. We were both his friends."

"Friends keep in touch," the woman said. "You been in touch with Odell?"

"No," Joe admitted. He was suddenly ashamed of himself for not staying in touch.

"If you'd kept in touch," the woman said accusingly, "you'd know Odell was gone." Her dark eyes turned wet. "Odell killed himself. My last born baby boy, went crazy and killed himself over those ugly lumps that growed all over his body—"

Suddenly Billy staggered back, stumbled off the top step, and fell to his knees. Joe tried to catch him, but missed. None of the three black youths moved to help.

"What's the matter with him?" the woman in the window asked.

"Same thing that was the matter with Odell," Joe told her.

The woman snapped her fingers at the three youths. "Y'all pick up that white boy and bring him in here," she ordered.

They hurried over to help.

Billy lived through the day, not dying until that night. Joe and Odell's mother, Olive Sampson, sat with him during his final hours. Olive held his hand.

"I'm sorry I didn't keep writing to Odell," Billy said quietly. "I tried writing to him, and he tried writing back, but we just didn't have nothing to say. Over in 'Nam we were *good* friends, *close* friends, 'cause we was both the same: both grunts, both trying to stay alive, both trying to make it through our tour and get back to the real world. Then when we did get back, we was different again. Odell was a big city, northern black man, and I was a small town, southern white man. We didn't have nothing to say to one another no more."

Olive Sampson nodded her head sadly. "I understand. I'm sure Odell did too. Don't you fret about it."

Delirium came and went as Billy lay there. Sometimes when he opened his eyes, he would look at Joe and say, "One more day. What would it have mattered, Joe? The goddamned war wasn't going nowhere, was it? Was it, Joe?"

"No, Billy, it wasn't," Joe quietly replied.

Billy looked at Olive. "Once we stopped killing other men, me and Odell didn't have nothing in common no more. That's sad, ain't it, Miz Olive?"

"Yes, son, that's sad," Olive agreed, her tears proving it.

It was twilight when Billy closed his eyes for the last time. Joe was alone in the room with him. Before he died, Billy clutched Joe's hand in the desperation of a last moment. "Make somebody pay, Joe," he pleaded. "For Chief Charlie and Odell and me. Make somebody pay."

Before Joe could answer, Billy was dead. Olive came back in and began to cry. "This is the same bed that my baby Odell went to his final peace on after he took all those awful pills they gave him."

"What pills? Who gave him?" Joe asked.

"Those folks at the veterans hospital. Odell kept going to see them, kept telling them there was something the matter with him from the war. They kept saying there wasn't nothing they could do for him, that there wasn't no proof that the war caused all those lumps on his body. When he got more and more lumps, he started pestering them every day. They finally started giving him tranquilizers to keep him calm.

Odell, why, he saved the pills up. We found five empty bottles on the sink."

Joe put his face in his hands. Olive Sampson came around the bed and stroked his head.

"Now, now. Don't you fret. Why, Billy and Odell are in a place where they can be friends again."

Joe started to cry a little. Billy's words came back to him again. *Make somebody pay, Joe.*

The memory of the words dried Joe's tears.

Olive Sampson promised to take charge of Billy's funeral and see that the V. A. buried him in the veterans cemetery where Odell was buried.

Joe left Chicago heading east. He drove until he was exhausted, then checked into a motel somewhere in Pennsylvania. He bought some takeout food and a bottle of gin, took a shower, turned on the television, ate, drank, turned off the television, and later, half drunk, went through Billy's suitcase. Besides the few clothes and a shave kit, Joe found Billy's service insurance policy for ten thousand dollars, with himself as the beneficiary. He also found a few photos of their fire team taken while they were still in Vietnam. The faces in the photos were all very young—Chief Charlie, Billy, Odell, himself. In one photo they were smiling, in another they were trying to look mean. Badass Marines. There was also a photo showing them with Lieutenant Russo, the platoon leader, and Colonel Lightman, the commanding officer. Billy had drawn a circle around Lightman's face—with orange crayon.

In the bottom of the suitcase, Joe found Billy's pistol: a .45 Colt that Billy had carried during his combat tour and stolen from the Marine Corps when he was discharged. It had walnut grips into which Billy, like a gunfighter of old, had carved a notch for every man he killed. Joe counted the notches. Forty of them. Billy's body count had been the second highest in the fire team. As Joe held the weapon, Billy's words returned again. *Make somebody pay*—

Joe slept that night with the gun and the picture of Lightman under his pillow.

The next morning, before he checked out, Joe used a sheet of motel stationery to sign over Billy's service insurance policy to Luz, Chief Charlie's sister. Joe had let his own service insurance policy lapse long ago—just, he thought, as he had let a lot of other things lapse: his pride, his self-respect, his guts.

But that was going to change now, he told himself, hefting Billy's pistol. One more notch was going to be carved on those walnut grips, one more number added to the fire team's body count.

Somebody was going to pay.

Joe drove on to Washington, D. C., and went to the records section at Marine Corps Headquarters. He showed his Reserve identification card to a pixieish woman Marine corporal. "Some of the guys from our outfit in 'Nam are organizing a reunion," he told her. "We thought it might be a nice touch to invite our old commanding officer." Joe shrugged good-naturedly. "He probably won't come; you know how officers are. But we'd like to send him an invitation anyway, if we can find out where he's at. His name is Colonel Ralph Lightman."

The corporal worked some keys on a computer terminal. After a moment she said, "Okay, here he is. Maybe he will come to your reunion, Sergeant; he lives right over in Virginia. Retired two years ago." She wrote down an address. "Good luck with the reunion."

"Thanks," Joe said, smiling. He put the address in his

The Color of Death

pocket next to the photo of Lightman with his face circled in orange crayon.

Traffic was heavy getting out of Washington and Joe did not reach the little Virginia suburb until after dark. At the address he had been given, he found a two-story red brick home set on a manicured lawn bordered by a horseshoe driveway. Parking down the road, Joe got Billy's pistol out of the glove compartment. He jacked a round into the chamber, carefully let the hammer back down, and put the gun on his hip under his belt, leaving his coat unbuttoned to avoid creating a bulge. Leaving his car, he walked back to the drive, keeping in shadows, stepping quietly. He glanced around for observers, at the same time trying to generate some saliva in a mouth suddenly gone dry. It had been a long time since he stalked an enemy. He heard a dog bark and was relieved to realize that it was not close. A light evening breeze brought with it a faint sound of soft music. Sweat broke out on his upper lip.

At the front door, Joe had to ring only once to get a response. The door was opened by a woman close to Joe's age, a plain woman without makeup, with plain hair pulled back and held somehow, dressed in tweed slacks and an old sweater. "Yes?" she asked, squinting at him in the porch light.

"Excuse me," Joe said. "Does Ralph Lightman live here?"

"Yes."

"Colonel Lightman?"

"Retired colonel, yes."

"I wonder if I could see him for a minute?" Joe asked. "I served under him in Vietnam. Some of us are organizing a reunion and we—"

"Please come in," the woman said, opening the door wider. "I'm Regina Arnold, the colonel's daughter."

"Is the colonel at home?" Joe asked, entering the foyer.

"Yes, he is." She tilted her head an inch, curiously. "Your name is—?"

Joe stared at her for a second. What the hell, he decided, he really didn't care whether he got caught or not. As a matter of fact, it would be *better* if he got caught: he could tell the press why he had done it. "Page," he answered. "Joe Page. I was a sergeant."

"And you're organizing a reunion?" The curiosity was edging toward suspicion.

"Yes. A reunion."

Regina Arnold studied him for a moment, seeming to ponder, then said, "All right. Follow me, please."

From the foyer she led him along a main floor hall to a pair of oak doors where she knocked softly before opening one. Joe followed her into the room. It was dark inside except for the glow of a large television in one corner. The sound emanating from the television was faint but instantly recognizable to Joe: small arms fire, grenade concussions, mortar explosions. When his eyes came round to the screen he saw news coverage of Vietnam combat action being shown from a video player. A figure sat hunched in front of the set. Joe's expression tightened. The old ghoul was reminiscing. Slipping the automatic from under his coat, Joe held it next to his leg, thumb on the hammer, finger on the trigger.

"Father," Regina Arnold said. "There's someone here. A sergeant named Joe Page."

The hunched figure looked over his shoulder at the lighted doorway. "Another one?"

"I'm not sure, Father."

Joe saw a hand move and the television became silent, reducing its violent images to a dreamlike quality. The hand moved farther and turned on a lamp. Then the figure whirled around and moved forward and Joe saw that the chair was a wheelchair. Squinting in the new light, his eyes fell on the face of Ralph Lightman. The same face that Billy had circled in orange crayon. A face now covered with fatty lumps, as if it had been pushed into a hive and stung by a hundred bees. The hideous countenance looked up at Joe.

"How do you intend to do it, Sergeant? Bayonet? Pistol? Grenade?"

Joe glanced at Regina Arnold. She was staring fiercely at him. His mouth was dry again, but his palm next to the pistol grip was moist. Inside, he felt the once-familiar sensation that Marines called "combat guts"—the tickling, tingling, feeling that first mushroomed in a man's stomach, then trickled into his legs, and finally backed up into his groin, like a reverse orgasm, weakening him the same way, suddenly, irreversibly. It took every nerve at his command just to swallow.

"Go ahead and do it," Lightman challenged. "I've been trying to get one of you to do it for a long time."

Make somebody pay, Joe—

Regina Arnold put a hand on Joe's arm. "Do it," she said.

Joe locked eyes with her. The woman's expression was intense and desperate, her face empty of color, ghostly.

"Put him to rest, for God's sake—" Her voice broke then and she looked away.

Make somebody pay—

Joe blinked rapidly several times, before shaking his head once in a quick jerk. Putting the gun back in his belt, he walked out of the room.

He was past the front door, crossing the drive, when Regina Arnold came running after him.

"Wait, please. I didn't mean what I said in there. It's just that he's suffered so long—"

Joe stopped and looked at her. The fierceness was gone from her eyes. There was something familiar, almost comfortable about her now, as if he'd known her plain face and tweeds and old sweater for a long time.

"Listen, you don't have to go," she said. "There's a place for you here."

Joe said nothing, but it was enough.

"Come," she urged, taking his hand, "let me show you."

Regina led him back into the big house and to another door that opened down a flight of stairs to the basement. There were no windows at that level but it was brightly lighted by fluorescents. Joe's lips parted incredulously as he looked at an arrangement of a dozen military bunk-beds, lockers, shelves—exactly like a barracks. Seven or eight men, some with visible fatty lumps, some without, were spread about the room reading, playing cards, watching television. One man, at a desk, was typing on an old portable.

A graying, heavyset black man got up from his bunk where he had been reading, removed his eyeglasses, and asked, "Name and rank?"

"Page," Joe said, wetting his lips, "Sergeant."

"I'm Moses, Master Sergeant," the black man said. "Put your weapon over there."

Looking where Moses indicated, Joe saw a small table on which lay an assortment of handguns, two bayonets, and one shrapnel grenade. Joe frowned and his jaw set slightly; reaching under his coat, he closed his hand on the automatic but did not relinquish it. Regina, who still held his hand, squeezed it gently.

"It's all right, Joe," she said quietly. "They all came here for the same reason you did: to make someone pay. And like you they realized it couldn't be done. There's no way anyone can *pay*. We can only learn." She nodded toward the man at the typewriter. "They're all telling their stories, Joe; they're being recorded for history. You can tell yours also."

The Color of Death

Not my story, Joe thought. Billy's story, and Chief Charles's and Odell's. *Their* story.

Joe put Billy's pistol on the table.

Moses held out his hand. "Welcome, brother."

An explanation of the term "Crowded Lives" was given in the INTRODUCTION *at the beginning of this collection. The story that follows was the inspiration for that title . . .*

Crowded Lives

George Simms stood across the street on Sixth Avenue and looked at the old Algiers Hotel. It did not appear markedly different than he remembered it from years earlier. There were a couple of vagrants loitering outside and a few scruffy kids playing where previously a uniformed doorman would never have allowed, but the vagrants and kids were there because the neighborhood had gone so far downhill. The hotel itself, twelve stories tall, standing formidably behind its marqueed entrance, was outwardly unchanged, as if its dignity, its style, might still be intact. George Simms knew, however, that inside would be a different story entirely.

When there was a lull in traffic, Simms crossed the street and tried five of the eight doors before he found one unlocked. Walking quietly across a marble floor, he stopped at the edge of the foyer and looked at the lobby. The Italian marble columns were still there, and some leaded windows high up in the wall that faced an inner courtyard, but that was all that remained unscathed. Most of the mahogany wainscoting and pilasters was warped, scarred, or broken off. The velvet tapestries were dusty and torn. The carpeting was worn, ripped, curling up in the corners. A lot of the original lobby furniture was still there, overstuffed chairs and divans on which stylishly dressed women had once taken afternoon tea. The women sitting on them now, George Simms observed, wore sweatshirts and Levi's and drank their coffee out of cardboard cups. Their children, perhaps two dozen of them, like their mothers of various colors, were playing on the worn carpet, hiding behind the torn tapestries, scribbling on the mahogany with stubs of crayon. Off in the corners sat a few elderly persons who watched them silently.

Across the foyer, a stout, uniformed woman sat at an incongruous green metal desk under a sign that read: ALL VISITORS MUST SIGN IN AND OUT. She had been watching Simms since he had walked in, and finally said, "Can I help you?"

Simms went over to her. "I'm supposed to go to work for Charlie Hosey."

"You from the halfway house?"

"Yes."

"Okay, you got to see Max Wallace first. He's head of security on the premises. See the grand ballroom over there; those big doors that are chained shut? Go down the hall next to them; you'll see his office."

Simms threaded his way through the playing children, past the women whose conversation ceased as he went by, past the big ballroom doors which did indeed have a length of chain connected to their brass handles by a padlock, and down a hall to a door that had ASSISTANT MANAGER lettered into its mahogany surface and a plastic sign reading "Security" thumb-tacked above it.

A black man dressed in starched, creased khaki, Max Wallace was thick but not fat, built like a fire hydrant, with eyes that riveted wherever they focused. As soon as Simms entered, they riveted on him. "Let's see your assignment paper," he said without preliminary.

Simms hesitated. "The job counselor at the halfway house said I was supposed to give that to Charlie Hosey."

"I don't care what the *job counselor* at the *halfway house* told you, bud. *I* am in charge of these premises, not him, and I want to see your assignment paper—*now.*" He held out a thick hand that matched the rest of him. Simms gave him the folded paper he wanted. Wallace's laser eyes flicked over it. "General maintenance man," he read, and grunted contemptuously. He tossed the paper back to Simms. "What'd you serve time for, Simms?" he asked, leaning forward, his words almost a challenge.

"You're not allowed to ask me that," Sims told him.

Wallace's eyes flashed anger, but just for an instant. He sat back. "They tell you that at the *halfway house?*" he asked, scornfully emphasizing the last two words.

"Yes." Simms wished he had a drink of water.

"Then I guess you also know that I can't ask *where* you did your time, or even how *much* time you did, that right?"

"Yes. Right."

"Well, since I'm not allowed to know anything about *you,* I'm going to tell you a few things about me. First of all, understand one thing: I am in charge of every*thing* and every*body* inside these premises. The Algiers is a city welfare hotel. There are nearly three hundred indigent families living here, many of them made up of women with young children." Wallace tilted his head with a coyness surprising for his size. "I guess you been away from women for quite a spell, haven't you?" Simms did not say anything. Wallace's eyes narrowed. "Couldn't be that you were away for rape, could it, Simms? I mean, it would be just like those halfway house fools to put a rapist in a building full of women to try to prove that he's been *re-ha-bil-i-tated.* Is that it, Simms? You a rapo?"

"I told you, you're not allowed to—"

"I heard you the first time!" Wallace stormed, slamming a big hand loudly on the desk. Leaning forward again, he pointed a threatening finger. "Every woman in this building is under my protection, Simms. I catch you out of line with any of them, you even look down one of their blouses when they bend over, and I'll have your ass back in the slammer so quick you'll think you never got out! Understand me?"

"I understand," Simms said quietly. Now he not only wanted a drink of water, he had to go to the bathroom too. He was very relieved when Wallace looked away long enough to pick up the phone and dial two digits.

"Charlie, this is Max," he said. "Come to my office and get your new helper."

When Wallace hung up, he sat far back in his swivel chair, the springs squeaking with the weight of him, and carefully unwrapped a large, black cigar that could have been designed with him in mind. Lighting it with an old-fashioned flip-top Zippo, he released puffs of pungent smoke into the air of the close little office. As he removed the cigar from his teeth, he actually smiled.

"Maybe I misjudged you, Simms," he said almost pleasantly. "Maybe you're not a rapo, after all." His smile, there for mere seconds, vanished, and his voice turned harsh again. "Maybe you're a goddamned child molester. A pervert. Is that what you are, Simms?"

George Simms did not have to worry about answering that one, because at that moment Charlie Hosey walked in.

"I can really use you," Hosey said as he showed Simms around the hotel. He was an older, short, balding man with a vague whiskey smell about him. "It ain't bad keeping up with the big stuff—the boiler, the hot water heaters, the electrical systems; it's the little stuff that runs me ragged. You know, the minor plumbing repairs, jammed locks, hot plates that are shorted out, lighting fixtures that don't work. You can handle all that kinda stuff, can't you?"

"Sure," Simms said. "Those are the same problems I used to take care of in the cellhouse. Except for jammed locks, that is; I wasn't allowed to mess with locks."

"I guess not," Hosey said, laughing.

"Did you come here through the halfway house too?" Simms asked.

"Me? No. I used to work here when the Algiers was a *real* hotel. I was maintenance superintendent when the place closed down. After that I went to St. Luke's Hospital for a few years. Then when I seen in the paper where the city was gonna lease the Algiers as a welfare hotel, I went and seen about coming back. They was glad to get me, I'll tell you. Keeping this place going is like working in a secondhand tire shop: it's patch, patch, patch all the time." They paused at the chained doors. "That's the Moroccan Ballroom," Hosey said. "The Duke and Duchess of Windsor used to throw parties in there. I seen 'em. It's got picnic tables in it now; the Help for the Homeless people come in twice a day and serve free meals. Over here," the little man led Simms across the lobby to a pair of locked leather-padded doors, "is the Casablanca Club. Used to be a real ritzy nightclub. All the big show people used to perform in there: Jolson, Helen Morgan, Blossom Seeley and Bennie Fields, Ruth Etting. I seen 'em." He sighed wistfully. "Yeah, this place used to be something."

They rode a service elevator, which Hosey had to unlock, down to the boiler room in the basement. On the way down, Simms asked, "What's with this guy Wallace anyway? He comes on like a concentration camp guard."

"Ex-cop," Hosey said. "Takes his job *real* serious." After a beat to think it over, he added, "Guess I ought to tell you: Max don't much like the halfway house sending guys to work here. You're the third one they sent; the other two didn't last long. Max, he don't give a guy much slack. He particularly don't like nobody messing around with none of the young women that lives here." Hosey shrugged. "I ain't telling you what to do, understand; but you asked and I thought you should know."

"Thanks," said Simms. "I appreciate it."

Off the big boiler room was the maintenance office: a badly scarred wooden desk littered with papers and miscellaneous junk, in front of a padded chair that had a patch repaired with black electrical tape. A wooden straight chair stood in front of the desk, an old metal file cabinet next to it. A pin-up girl calendar from a plumbing supply company was thumbtacked to the wall. At the back of the office was a curtained doorway leading to a small storeroom. The curtain was not closed all the way and Simms caught a glimpse of a cot in the room. He did not ask about it.

"Here's where I list all the minor repairs to be done," Hosey said, showing Simms a clipboard hanging on a nail. "Every day you just go down the list and do as many of 'em as you can. I ain't gonna dog you as long as you do a reasonable amount of work; I know all's you're getting is minimum wage for now. But if you work out and want a permanent job when you're released from the halfway house, why, we can talk about it."

"I'll do a good job for you, Mr. Hosey," Simms told him.

"Just call me Charlie," said the little man.

A week later, Simms was sitting on the fire stairs at the end of the seventh floor corridor, having a smoke and drinking coffee from a small thermos he had bought. His tool belt and the clipboard of job orders lay on the step next to him. He had been sitting there for nearly an hour. Finally the door to room 704 opened and a little Puerto Rican girl, five or six years old, came out into the corridor to play. Pretty, clay-colored, with raven hair, she had on jeans and a sweater, and carried a doll that was missing a hand. Sitting on the worn carpet with her back to the wall, the child propped up her knees, sat the doll on them, and began to braid the doll's hair.

Simms watched her for a couple of minutes, then leaned forward a little and spoke to her. "Hello." He said it very quietly so as not to frighten her.

She looked at him but did not speak back.

"My name's George," he said. "I work here." He showed her the tool belt. "See?"

The little girl looked, then turned her attention back to the doll.

"That sure is a pretty doll," Simms said. "But what happened to her hand?"

"She was in a accident," the child said, not looking at him.

"That's too bad," Simms said consolingly. "But she's a very lucky little doll to have you to take care of her." From the pocket of his denim work shirt, Simms took a pack of chewing gum. Slowly unwrapping a stick, he put it in his mouth. He knew the little girl was watching him. "Would you like some gum?" he asked. She looked back at her doll without answering. "It's fruit flavored," he said. "Sure is good. Here," he held out a stick, "have some—"

The girl rose and walked over to him. She stood before the stairs he was sitting on and Simms gave her the gum and watched as she unwrapped it and put it in her mouth. As she began to chew, she smiled.

"See, told you it was good," Simms said. A lock of hair had fallen over her forehead and Simms reached out and brushed it back. "I told you my name, but if we're going to be friends you've got to tell me yours—"

Just then a woman came out of 704 and strode urgently over to them. "Debbie, what are you *doing?*" she said irritably.

Simms frowned. Debbie? *Debbie?* What the hell kind of name was that for a Puerto Rican kid?

The woman took the girl by one arm. "You know you're supposed to stay right by the door! And not talk to strangers!"

"It's okay," Simms said, smiling. "I work here."

"I don't give a damn where you work, mister!" the woman snapped. She was pretty, an older version of the child, except that her eyes had no innocence left in them. "What have you got in your mouth?" she demanded of Debbie. "Spit it out," she ordered, holding her hand under the child's mouth. "Now get back in the room!" As the little girl hurried away, the woman turned her anger on Simms. "What the hell do you think you're doing, giving gum to my kid? Who the hell are you anyway?"

"My name's George," Simms said, shrugging. "I work here." He held up the tool belt. "I fix things."

"Yeah, well if I ever catch you giving anything to my kid again, I'm gonna *fix* you," the woman threatened. She stuck the wad of gum on the handle of his screwdriver. "Stay away from my kid, mister!"

She stalked away.

A few days later, Simms went down to the maintenance office for some new work orders, and Hosey was not at his desk. Simms pulled the curtain aside and looked into the storeroom for him. He was not there either. It was the first time Simms had seen the storeroom except for an occasional glimpse when the curtains were left open an inch or so. Now he looked around curiously. The cot that he had seen his first day there was of the ordinary folding variety, with a blue-striped mattress and a couple of gray blankets that had ST. LUKE HOSPITAL printed on them. An upturned wooden crate served as a nightstand; on it was a cheap little lamp, an ash tray full of cigarette butts, and a glossy porno magazine with a nude woman in bondage on the cover. Standing on the floor next to the cot was an almost empty Jim Beam bottle. A few of Hosey's extra clothes hung from nails in the wall.

The phone on Hosey's desk rang. Simms closed the curtain and answered it. "Maintenance."

"Where's Charlie?"

Simms recognized Max Wallace's voice. "I don't know, I just walked in."

"Find him," Wallace ordered crisply. "Then the two of you get up to my office—*fast*."

Simms found Hosey over in a section of the basement that had been converted into a laundry room for the welfare tenants. He had the drum out of a clothes dryer and was resetting its axle. Simms told him about Wallace's call and Hosey put aside his work.

"Did he say what it was about?" the little man asked.

"No," said Simms. "He just sounded mad—as usual."

When they got to the security office, Max Wallace was with a little black girl of eight or nine and her mother. Wallace glanced at Hosey, glared at Simms, and knelt in front of the girl. "Sweetheart, I want you to look at these two men and tell me if it was either one of them that scared you." The child hesitated and Wallace gently patted her head. "It's all right, come on now, take a look for me."

The little girl looked at Hosey and Simms, frowned, seemed to ponder, and finally said, "I'm not sure. It was so dark—" Her voice broke and she whimpered a little. Wallace gestured to her mother.

"I'll talk to her again later. Meantime, try to go on with her normal routine as much as you can. Don't avoid the subject but don't talk about it like it was the end of the world either. Understand?"

"Yes, all right," the mother replied in a strained voice. She took her daughter and left.

Wallace sat behind his desk and studied Hosey and Simms with cold eyes. "That little girl," he said evenly, "was on her way down the stairs to go to school this morning when a man accosted her on the landing between the lobby and two. She says the man tried to kiss her. The light on the landing was out, but she saw that he was a white man and she says he had a funny smell—"

"Well, why pick on us?" Charlie Hosey said indignantly.

"You're white and you're in the building," Wallace said.

"For Christ's sake, there's prob'ly two or three dozen white guys *living* in the place," Hosey argued. "And there's boyfriends that sneak in and spend the night, there's johns that some of these women go out and pick up for extra money—you got no right to single us out, Wallace." The little maintenance man was decidedly irate.

"Nobody said I was singling you out; I always check the obvious first." The security man reached for his phone. "You can go," he told them.

His eyes lingered on Simms until he was out the door.

That afternoon, Simms was helping Hosey rehang one of the lobby doors that the kids had misaligned by swinging on it.

"Maybe I shouldn't have got so hot at Max," the little man mused. "He's just trying to do his job. It ain't an easy one either, I'll tell you. There's lots going on in this place that shouldn't be going on: prostitution, drug sales, stolen property being sold—"

"I guess you never expected to see those kind of things in the Algiers," Simms commented.

"Not stuff like that, never," Hosey declared. "Course, in

any big city hotel you're gonna get your share of illegal goings-on. Hell, I used to see Meyer Lansky and Lucky Luciano come in here regular to have a drink in the Oasis Bar; there's no telling what kind of crooked business they was talking about. And one time we found out there was a high price call girl ring operating out of what used to be the penthouse suite. It was supposed to be rented to this wealthy Texas dame and her four daughters; well, they wasn't her daughters at all, if you know what I mean." Hosey grinned. "Funniest thing that ever happened was the time some teller over at Chase Manhattan got conned by a blonde who was a dead ringer for Lana Turner. She was supposed to run away with him, see, after he embezzled a bundle of dough, but what she really did was run away *from* him—*with* the dough. Cops arrested him right here in the hotel, sitting on the bed, suitcase all packed, waiting for her to come back."

While Hosey was talking, Simms noticed Debbie's mother go into the coffee shop across the street from the hotel. Debbie was not with her.

"She got caught later on," Hosey said.

"What?"

"The blonde that looked like Lana Turner. She got caught down in Florida somewheres. Only had about ten thousand dollars left. Claimed the bank teller only gave her twenty. The bank said a *hundred* thousand was stole. Ask me, the bankers prob'ly took the difference." Hosey used an electric drill on a long extension cord to screw in the last door hinge. "Well, that about does it. Wish there was some way to keep the kids from swinging on it, but I guess there ain't. We'll be fixing it again in a month."

"Okay if I take a few minutes off, Charlie?" Simms asked. He could see Debbie's mother sitting by the coffee shop window with a cup in front of her.

"Sure, take a break," Hosey said, winding up his extension cord.

Simms trotted over to the coffee shop and went up to the table where Debbie's mother sat. "Can I talk to you a minute?" he asked.

She looked up from a folded section of classified ads. "What about?"

Simms sat across from her. "I just wanted to tell you I was sorry for what happened about the gum. I guess I wasn't thinking. I mean, it was just a natural thing to offer the kid a stick of gum. It never occurred to me how it might look."

"Just stay away from my kid, okay?" the woman said firmly.

"Yeah, sure I will," Simms assured. "I just wanted you to know I didn't mean nothing by it. I was only trying to be friendly."

"Okay, but don't let it happen again." She sighed wearily. "That place over there," she bobbed her chin at the hotel, "is a sewer. A mother with a kid, she can't be too careful."

"I know, I realize that now. I'm sorry, okay?" He took a pack of gum from his shirt pocket. "How about you?" he asked, raising his eyebrows. "You want a stick of gum?"

She half smiled in spite of herself. "Why not?" She took a stick and put it in her mouth.

"Looking for a job?" Simms asked, nodding at the classifieds.

"Yeah. Soon's I find one, I'm getting out of that dump over there."

"Listen," he told her, "I go to this place at night, it's kind of a community center, and sometimes I hear about job openings over there. If I hear of anything I think might interest you, I'll let you know."

Her eyes flashed suspicion. "What do you think that'll get you?"

"What do you mean?"

"I don't sleep around, man, if you're looking to score."

"Hey," Simms said righteously, "I'm just trying to be a nice guy. Lighten up a little."

She sighed again. "Well, you just never know. Seems like everybody's out to get something."

"I know," he sympathized. "It's hard to tell who's being straight with you sometimes." Simms drummed his fingers on the tabletop. After a moment, he asked, "So where's Debbie?"

"She's in daycare until three."

"Say, how'd you ever happen to give her a name like Debbie?" he asked. "I mean, that's kind of an all-*American* girl-next-door name."

"Maybe I'd like her to grow up to be an all-American girl next door." There was a hint of defiance in her words. "Anything wrong with that?"

"No, not at all. Listen, no offense intended," he said quickly. "Hey, speaking of names, what's yours?"

"Lupe Mercado," she told him.

"I'm George Simms," he said. He extended his hand and, after first hesitating, she shook it.

"If you ever need anything fixed in your room," he said, "just let me know; you don't have to fill out a form and wait your turn, I'll do it for you right away."

Lupe shrugged. "Okay." There was a tiny pinch at the top of her nose.

"I better be getting back," Simms said, rising. "Thanks for not being mad at me anymore."

Outside, as he waited to cross the street, Simms looked back and saw her watching him suspiciously. He smiled and

Crowded Lives

waved. She still doesn't trust me all that much, he thought. But for his purposes, that was okay.

All he needed was a *little* trust.

For a week Simms watched Lupe Mercado come and go. Her routine never varied. First thing in the morning she took Debbie to daycare, then spent the rest of the morning job-hunting. Usually at noon she was back at the hotel for the free meal served by Help for the Homeless. After lunch she would sit in the lobby or go across to the coffee shop and read the classifieds again to see if there was anything she missed that morning. Sometimes Simms would see her using one of the pay phones in the lobby to call about jobs. Just before three she would leave to go get her daughter from daycare.

Now and then Simms would speak to her in passing, or wave to her across the lobby, but he did not intrude on what she was doing, encroach on her time, or in any way act as if he was presuming a friendship. All he wanted to do was keep her aware of him until he was ready.

He picked Thursday as the day. Thursday: late in the week when people were tired, not as alert, laboring toward the weekend. Simms had already selected the boiler room door that led to the alley as the way by which he would leave the hotel. He knew he would have to move fast; Max Wallace would be after him very quickly.

At three-thirty Simms was on the seventh floor when Lupe Mercado got off the elevator with Debbie and came down the corridor to 704. Simms pretended to be in a hurry.

"I was hoping I'd run into you," he said in a rush of words. "I only got a second; there's a bad leaky pipe in the basement I got to tend to." Fumbling in his pocket, he pulled out a slip of paper. "This lady's got a dress shop in the village. She wants somebody to work in her stockroom. Says she'll train somebody with no experience. Said it was good pay plus a discount on clothes. Give her a call as soon as you can; the job might still be open." Pressing the slip of paper into her hand, he said, "Listen, I've got to hurry; that pipe's leaking all over the basement. Hope you get the job."

Simms hurried down the corridor to the fire stairs. He made sure his footsteps sounded loudly as he ran down to six, and halfway down to five. Then he abruptly turned and crept quietly back up to seven. Standing just around the corner from the corridor, he heard Lupe Mercado speaking to her daughter.

"—phone in the lobby. I'll be just a few minutes. You *stay* inside until I get back. *Don't* play in the hall."

Hearing a door close, Simms peered around the corner. Lupe Mercado was hurrying back toward the elevator.

Simms waited until she got on the elevator, then walked quickly to 704. When he knocked, Debbie opened the door on a chain.

"Debbie," he said easily, "call your mother to the door; I gave her the wrong phone number."

"She went downstairs."

"Oh. Well, let me in and I'll wait for her. I have to give her the right number."

He took a pack of gum from his pocket and put a stick in his mouth.

"It's okay," he assured, "your mother and I are friends. You know I'm helping her find a job."

Unwrapping another stick of gum, he held it through the opening. Debbie hesitated. Then she took it. Simms unfolded several work orders he had stuck under his toolbelt.

"While I'm waiting, I want to check something in your bathroom that needs fixing." He added just a hint of firmness to his voice. "Open the door now, Debbie, so I can get to work."

Debbie took the chain off and opened the door. When Simms got inside, he closed and locked the door behind him.

In the lobby, Lupe hung up the telephone and stared at the slip of paper in confusion. It was the number of a dress shop in the Village, all right, but the sales clerk Lupe had talked to knew nothing of any stockroom job that was open. The clerk had called the manager to the phone, but the manager knew nothing about it either. And the owner of the store was out of town on a buying trip.

Puzzled, Lupe started back toward the elevators. Charlie Hosey was near the elevator bank, repairing a drinking fountain. Max Wallace had just walked up to him.

"Where's Simms?" Wallace asked the maintenance man.

"He went up to seven to do something," Hosey said. "He ain't come down yet."

Lupe stopped and stared at them. "Oh my god!" she said after several seconds.

"What's the matter?" asked Max Wallace.

Without answering, Lupe ran toward the elevators.

"Simms," Wallace said tightly. "I knew it!" He ran after Lupe.

Hosey ran after both of them.

In the bathroom of 704, Debbie was sitting on the edge of the tub, watching Simms in fascination. He had emptied the medicine cabinet of all its contents, piling them in the sink. Then, with a power screw remover, he had unscrewed four three-inch wood screws that held the metal medicine cabinet into the wall studs on each side of it. With a small chisel, Simms had pried loose the top, bottom, and both sides of the cabinet and taken it out of the wall. Then he had stuck his arm far down into the opening between walls and pulled up a pillowcase that had "Algiers Hotel" embroidered across its hem.

"Thanks, kid," he said, tucking the pillowcase under one arm. "Tell your mother to call maintenance to have this put back in."

Simms started for the door and Debbie quickly followed him. At the door, Simms paused and gave her the rest of the pack of gum. "Your mother's right, you know," he told her quietly. "You really shouldn't talk to strangers or take gum and stuff. Promise me you won't do it again?"

Smiling shyly, Debbie said, "I promise, George."

Simms opened the door and stepped into the corridor. Max Wallace, just hurrying up, put a gun in his face.

"Move a muscle and you're gone," he said coldly.

Simms froze. Lupe Mercado rushed past him to gather Debbie into her arms. "My baby! What did he do to you?" she cried.

"I didn't do anything to her—" Simms tried to protest.

"Shut up!" Wallace ordered.

Peering past Wallace's shoulder, Charlie Hosey's face brightened. "Now I remember you! You're the bank teller! I always thought you looked familiar—"

Wallace frowned. "That Chase Manhattan embezzler you told me about?"

"That's the one," said Hosey.

Wallace snatched the pillowcase from Simms and looked inside it. "Well, I'll be damned," he whispered.

"It must have been hidden in that room all these years," Hosey said. "Eighty thousand dollars."

Lupe Mercado stared at the bundles of currency in the open pillowcase, then turned her eyes incredulously to Simms, her lips parted in stunned disbelief. Wallace put handcuffs on Simms and started leading him away.

"Why didn't you tell me?" Lupe asked, following them down the hall, indignation rising. "We could have shared it! We could have both got out of the sewer! Why didn't you trust me enough to tell me?"

"Me, trust *you?*" Simms said. "You wouldn't even trust me enough to give your kid a stick of gum!"

In the middle of the corridor, Wallace pushed Simms onto the elevator. Lupe stood there helplessly.

"You could have *tried!*" she accused. Then more softly, "*I* could have tried—"

"Well, it's too late now," Simms said.

The elevator door closed them off from each other for the last time.

All stories reprinted by permission of the author.

"Introduction" Copyright © 2000 by Clark Howard.

"Old Soldier" Copyright © 1982 by Clark Howard.

"Hit and Run" Copyright © 1981 by Clark Howard.

"Wild Things" Copyright © 1983 by Clark Howard.

"McCulla's Kid" Copyright © 1985 by Clark Howard.

"Hanging It on a Limb" Copyright © 1989 by Clark Howard.

"New Orleans Getaway" Copyright © 1983 by Clark Howard.

"The Marksman" Copyright © 1967 by Clark Howard.

"The Color of Death" Copyright © 1988 by Clark Howard.

"Crowded Lives" Copyright © 1989 by Clark Howard.